KILLING ORDERS

G·K Hall &Cº

Also published in Large Print
from G.K. Hall by Sara Paretsky:

Deadlock
Indemnity Only
Bitter Medicine
A Woman's Eye
Guardian Angel
Blood Shot
Burn Marks

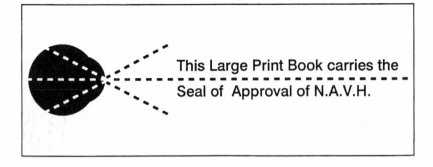

This Large Print Book carries the
Seal of Approval of N.A.V.H.

KILLING ORDERS

Sara Paretsky

G.K. Hall & Co.
Thorndike, Maine

Published in Large Print by arrangement with
William Morrow & Co., Inc.

G.K. Hall Large Print Book Series.

Set in 16 pt. News Plantin.

Printed on acid free paper in the United States of America.

Library of Congress Cataloging-in-Publication Data

Paretsky, Sara.
    Killing orders / Sara Paretsky.
      p. cm.
    ISBN 0-8161-5598-4 (alk. paper : lg. print).—
    ISBN 0-8161-5599-2 (alk. paper : lg. print : pbk).
    1. Warshawski, V.I. (Fictitious character)—Fiction. 2. Private
investigators—Illinois—Chicago—Fiction. 3. Women detectives—
Illinois—Chicago—Fiction. 4. Chicago (Ill.)—Fiction. 5. Large
type books. I. Title.
    [PS3566.A647K5 1993]
    813'.54—dc20   93-13221
                                                           CIP

For Courtenay
All other things to their destruction draw

Acknowledgments

Thanks to Bill Tiritilli, director of research for the brokerage firm Rodam and Renshaw, for advice on law and practice in takeovers of publicly held companies.

Marilyn Martin, J.D., is a public defender. Unlike V.I. Warshawski, she has not allowed the discouragements of the job to stop her from practicing it. She supplied me with information about the Illinois criminal code, probable grounds for arrest, and about Chicago's Women's Court. Any mistakes are due to my ignorance, not her information.

Kimball Wright, enraged by repeated errors regarding the Smith & Wesson in V.I.'s previous adventures, provided me with better information about the weapon.

The Reverend Albertus Magnus, O.P., has often allowed me the great pleasure of visiting him and his brother Dominicans at the House of Studies in Washington. Because I know this order better than any other, I chose it as part of the setting for this story. The Priory of Albertus Magnus in Chicago is totally fictitious, as are the friars who reside there.

And many thanks, too, to James H. Lorie.

Contents

I

Old Wounds

My stomach muscles contracted as I locked the car door. I hadn't been to Melrose Park for ten years, but, as I walked up the narrow pavement to the house's side entrance, I felt a decade of maturity slipping from me, felt the familiar sickening, my heart thudding.

The January wind scattered dead leaves around my feet. Little snow had fallen this winter, but the air blew cold. After ringing the bell I jammed my hands deep into the pockets of my navy car coat to keep them warm. I tried to argue my nervousness away. After all, they had called me . . . begged me for help. . . . The words meant nothing. I had lost an important battle by responding to the plea.

I stamped my feet to loosen the toes frozen inside thin-soled loafers and heard, at last, a rattling behind the painted blue door. It swung inward into a dimly lit vestibule. Through the screen I could just make out my cousin Albert, much heavier than he'd been ten years ago. The screen and the dark behind him softened his pout.

"Come in, Victoria. Mother is waiting for you."

I bit back an excuse for being a quarter hour late and turned it into a neutral comment on the

9

weather. Albert was almost bald, I noted with pleasure. He took my coat ungraciously and draped
it over the banister at the foot of the narrow, uncarpeted stairs.

A deep, harsh voice called to us. "Albert! Is
that Victoria?"

"Yes, Mama," Albert muttered.

The only light in the entryway came from a tiny
round window facing the stairs. The dimness ob-
scured the pattern in the wallpaper, but as I followed Albert down the close corridor I could see
it hadn't changed; gray paper with white loops,
ugly, cold. As a child, I thought the paper oozed
hate. Behind Albert's wobbling thighs the old chill
stuck out tendrils at me and I shivered.

I used to beg my mother, Gabriella, not to bring
me to this house. Why should we go? Rosa hated
her, hated me, and Gabriella always cried after
the long L ride home. But she would only set her
lips in a tight smile and say, "I am obligated, *cara*.
I must go."

Albert led me into the formal parlor at the back
of the house. The horsehair furniture was as familiar to me as my own apartment. In my night-
mares I dreamed of being trapped in this room
with its stiff furniture, the ice-blue drapes, the
sad picture of Uncle Carl over the fake fireplace,
and Rosa, thin, hawk-nosed, frowning, seated
poker-backed in a spindle-legged chair.

Her black hair was iron-colored now, but the
severe, disapproving stare was unaltered. I tried
taking diaphragm breaths to calm the churning in

my stomach. You're here because *she* begged *you,* I reminded myself.

She didn't stand up, didn't smile — I couldn't remember ever seeing her smile. "It was good of you to come, Victoria." Her tone implied it would have been better if I'd come on time. "When one is old, one doesn't travel easily. And the last few days have made me old indeed."

I sat down in what I hoped was the least uncomfortable chair. "Yes," I said noncommittally. Rosa was about seventy-five. When they performed her autopsy, they would find her bones were made of cast iron. She did not look old to me: She hadn't begun to rust yet.

"Albert. Pour some coffee for Victoria."

Rosa's single virtue was her cooking. I took a cup of the rich Italian coffee gratefully, but ignored the tray of pastries Albert proffered — I'd get pastry cream on my black wool skirt and feel foolish as well as tense.

Albert sat uneasily on the narrow settee, eating a piece of *torta del re,* glancing surreptitiously at the floor when a crumb dropped, then at Rosa to see if she'd noticed.

"You are well, Victoria? You are happy?"

"Yes," I said firmly. "Both well and happy."

"But you have not remarried?"

The last time I'd been here was with my brief husband for a strained bridal visit. "It is possible to be happy and not married, as Albert doubtless can tell you, or as you know yourself." The last was a cruel remark: Uncle Carl had killed himself

11

shortly after Albert was born. I felt vindictively pleased, then guilty. Surely I was mature enough not to need that kind of satisfaction. Somehow Rosa always made me feel eight years old.

Rosa shrugged her thin shoulders disdainfully. "No doubt you are right. Yet for me — I am to die without the joy of grandchildren."

Albert shifted uncomfortably on the settee. It was clearly not a new complaint.

"A pity," I said. "I know grandchildren would be the crowning joy of a happy and virtuous life."

Albert choked but recovered. Rosa narrowed her eyes angrily. "You, of all people, should know why my life has not been happy."

Despite my efforts at control, anger spilled over. "Rosa, for some reason you think Gabriella destroyed your happiness. What mysterious grievance a girl of eighteen could have caused you I don't know. But you threw her out into the city on her own. She didn't speak English. She might have been killed. Whatever she did to you, it couldn't have been as bad as what you did to her.

"You know the only reason I'm here: Gabriella made me promise that I would help you if you needed it. It stuck in my gut and it still does. But I promised her, and here I am. So let's leave the past in peace: I won't be sarcastic if you'll stop throwing around insults about my mother. Why not just tell me what the problem is."

Rosa tightened her lips until they almost disappeared. "The most difficult thing I ever did in my life was to call you. And now I see I should not have done it." She rose in one movement, like a steel crane, and left the room. I could hear the angry clip of her shoes on the uncarpeted hall and up the bare stairs. In the distance a door slammed.

I put down my coffee and looked at Albert. He had turned red with discomfort, but he seemed less amorphous with Rosa out of the room.

"How bad is her trouble?"

He wiped his fingers on a napkin and folded it tidily. "Pretty bad," he muttered. "Why'd you have to make her mad?"

"It makes her mad to see me here instead of at the bottom of Lake Michigan. Every time I've talked to her since Gabriella died she's been hostile to me. If she needs help, all I want is the facts. She can save the rest for her psychiatrist. I don't get paid enough to deal with it." I picked up my shoulder bag and stood up. At the doorway I stopped and looked at him.

"I'm not coming back to Melrose Park for another round, Albert. If you want to tell me the story I'll listen. But if I leave now, that's it; I won't respond to any more pleas for family unity from Rosa. And by the way, if you do want to hire me, I'm not working out of love for your mother."

He stared at the ceiling, listening perhaps for guidance from above. Not heaven — just the back bedroom. We couldn't hear anything. Rosa was probably jabbing pins into a piece of clay with a lock of my hair stuck to it. I rubbed my arms involuntarily, searching for damage.

13

Albert shifted uneasily and stood up. "Uh, look, uh, maybe I'd better tell you."

"Fine. Can we go to a more comfortable room?"

"Sure. Sure." He gave a half smile, the first I'd seen that afternoon. I followed him back down the hall to a room on the left. It was tiny, but clearly his private spot. A giant set of stereo speakers loomed from one wall; below them were some built-in shelves holding an amplifier and a large collection of tapes and records. No books except a few accounting texts. His high-school trophies. A tiny cache of bottles.

He sat in the one chair, a large leather desk chair with a hassock next to it. He slid the hassock over to me and I perched on that.

In his own place, Albert relaxed and his face took on a more decisive look. He was a CPA with his own business, I remembered. When you saw him with Rosa, you couldn't imagine him managing anything on his own, but in here it didn't seem so improbable.

He took a pipe from the desk top next to him and began the pipe smoker's interminable ritual with it. With luck I'd be gone before he actually lit it. All smoke makes me ill, and pipe smoke on top of an empty stomach — I'd been too tense for lunch — would be disastrous.

"How long have you been a detective, Victoria?"

"About ten years." I swallowed my annoyance at being called Victoria. Not that it isn't my name. Just that if I liked using it I wouldn't go by my initials.

"And you're good at it?"

"Yes. Depending on your problem, I'm about the best you can get. . . . I have a list of references if you want to call someone."

"Yeah, I'd like a name or two before you go." He had finished drilling out the pipe bowl. He knocked it methodically against the side of an ashtray and began packing it with tobacco. "Mother's gotten herself involved with some counterfeit securities."

Wild dreams of Rosa as the brains behind Chicago's Mob ran through my head. I could see six-point screamer headlines in the *Herald-Star.*

"Involved how?"

"They found some in the St. Albert Priory safe."

I sighed to myself. Albert was deliberately going to drag this out. "She plant them there? What's she got to do with this priory?"

The moment of truth had come: Albert struck a match and began sucking on the pipestem. Sweet blue smoke curled up around his head and wafted toward me. I felt my stomach turn over.

"Mother's been their treasurer for the last twenty years. I thought you knew." He paused a minute to let me feel guilty about not keeping up with the family. "Of course they had to ask her to leave when they found the securities."

"Does she know anything about them?"

He shrugged. He was sure she didn't. He didn't know how many there were, what companies they were drawn on, how long since they'd last been examined, or who had access to them. The only thing he knew was the new prior wanted to sell them in order to make repairs on the building. Yes, they'd been in a safe.

"Her heart's broken because of the suspicion." He saw my derisive look and said defensively, "Just because you only see her when she's upset or angry you can't imagine she has real feelings. She's seventy-five, you know, and that job meant a lot to her. She wants her name cleared so she can go back."

"Surely the FBI is investigating, and the SEC."

"Yes, but they'd be just as happy to hang it on her if it made things easier for them. After all, who wants to take a priest to court? And they know she's old, she'd get off with a suspended sentence."

I blinked a few times. "Albert. No. You're out of touch. If she were some poor West Side black, they might railroad her. But not Rosa. She'd scare 'em too much for one thing. And the FBI — they'll want to get to the bottom of this. They're never going to believe an old woman masterminded a counterfeiting scheme." Unless, of course, she had. I wished I could believe it, but Rosa was malicious, not dishonest.

"But that church is the only thing she really loves," he blurted, turning crimson. "They might believe she got carried away. People do."

We talked about it some more, but it ended as I suppose I'd known it had to, with me pulling out two copies of my standard contract for Albert to sign. I gave him a family rate on the fee —

sixteen dollars an hour instead of twenty.

He told me the new prior would be expecting my call. Boniface Carroll his name was. Albert wrote that on a piece of paper along with a rough map of how to find the priory. I frowned as I stuck it in my bag. They were taking an awful lot for granted. Then I laughed sourly at myself. Once I'd agreed to make the trek to Melrose Park they could take a lot for granted.

Back at my car I stood rubbing my head for a few minutes, hoping the cold clean air would blow the pipe fumes from my throbbing brain. I glanced back at the house. A curtain fell quickly at an upstairs window. I climbed into the car somewhat cheered. To see Rosa spy furtively on me — like a small child or a thief — made me feel somehow that more of the power lay in my hands.

II

Remembrance of Things Past

I woke up sweating. The bedroom was dark and for a moment I couldn't remember where I was. Gabriella had been staring at me, her eyes huge in her wasted face, the skin translucent as it had been those last painful months of her life, pleading with me to help her. The dream had been in Italian. It took time to reorient myself to English, to adulthood, to my apartment.

The digital clock glowed faintly orange. Five-thirty. My sweat turned to a chill. I pulled the comforter up around my neck and clenched my teeth to keep them from chattering.

My mother died of cancer when I was fifteen. As the disease ate the vitality from her beautiful face, she made me promise to help Rosa if her aunt ever needed me. I had tried to argue with Gabriella: Rosa hated her, hated me — we had no obligation. But my mother insisted and I could not refuse.

My father had told me more than once how he met my mother. He was a policeman. Rosa had thrown Gabriella out on the street, an immigrant with minimal English. My mother, who always had more courage than common sense, was trying to earn a living doing the only thing she knew:

singing. Unfortunately, none of the Milwaukee Avenue bars where she auditioned liked Puccini or Verdi and my father rescued her one day from a group of men who were trying to force her to strip. Neither he nor I could understand why she ever saw Rosa again. But I made her the promise she wanted.

My pulse had calmed down but I knew more sleep was out of the question. Shivering in the cold room, I padded naked to the window and pulled back the heavy curtain. The winter morning was black. Snow falling like a fine mist glowed in the streetlamp at the corner of the alley. I kept shivering, but the still morning held me entranced, the thick black air pressing at me comfortingly.

At last I let the curtain drop. I had a ten o'clock meeting in Melrose Park with the new prior of St. Albert's. I might as well get going.

Even in the winter I try to run five miles a day. Although financial crime, my specialty, doesn't often lead to violence, I grew up in a rough South Side neighborhood where girls as well as boys had to be able to defend themselves. Old habits die hard, so I work out and run to stay in shape. Anyway, running is the best way I know to ward off the effects of pasta. I don't enjoy exercise, but it beats dieting.

In the winter I wear a light sweatshirt, loose pants, and a down vest. Once warmed up I donned these and ran quickly down the hall and three flights of stairs to keep my muscles loose.

Outside, I wanted to abandon the project. The

cold and damp were miserable. Even though the streets were already filling with early commuters, it was hours before my usual waking time, and the sky had barely begun to lighten by the time I got back to Halsted and Belmont. I walked carefully up the stairs to my apartment. The steps were shiny with age and very slippery when wet. I had a vision of myself sliding backward on wet running shoes, cracking my skull on old marble.

A long hallway divides my apartment in half and makes it seem bigger than its four rooms. The dining room and kitchen are to the left; bedroom and living room to the right. For some reason the kitchen connects to the bathroom. I turned on water for a shower and went next door to start coffee.

Armed with coffee, I took my running clothes off and sniffed them. Smelly, but not too bad for one more morning. I dropped them over a chair back and gave myself up to a long hot shower. The stream of water drumming on my skull soothed me. I relaxed, and without realizing it, I started to sing a bit under my breath. After a while the tune drifted into my consciousness, a sad Italian folksong Gabriella used to sing. Rosa was really lying heavy on my mind — the nightmare, visions of my skull breaking, now mournful songs. I was not going to let her control me this way — that would be the ultimate defeat. I shampooed my hair vigorously and forced myself to sing Brahms. I don't like his *Lieder*, but some, like "Meine Liebe Ist Grün," are almost painfully cheerful.

Coming out of the shower I switched to the dwarfs' song from *Snow White*. Off to work we go. My navy walking suit, I decided, to make me mature and dignified. It had a three-quarter-length double-breasted jacket and a skirt with two side pleats. A knit silk top of pale gold, almost the color of my skin, and a long scarf bright with red and navy and brushed again with the same gold. Perfect. I edged the corners of my eyes with a faint trace of blue pencil to make their gray color bluer, added a little light rouge and lipstick to match the red in the scarf. Open-toed red-leather pumps, Italian. Gabriella brought me up to believe that my feet would fall off if I wore shoes made anyplace else. Even now that a pair of Magli pumps go for a hundred forty dollars, I can't bring myself to wear Comfort-Stride.

I left the breakfast dishes in the sink with last night's supper plates and those from a few other meals. And the bed unmade. And the clothes strewn around. Perhaps I should save the money I spent on clothes and shoes and invest in a housekeeper. Or even a hypnosis program to teach me to be neat and tidy. But what the hell. Who besides me was going to see it?

III

The Order of Preachers

The Eisenhower Expressway is the main escape route from Chicago to the western suburbs. Even on warm sunny days, it looks like a prison exercise yard for most of its length. Run-down houses and faceless projects line the tops of the canyons on either side of its eight lanes. L stations are planted along the median. The Eisenhower is always choked with traffic, even at three in the morning. At nine on a wet workday it was impossible.

I could feel tension tightening the cords in the back of my neck as I oozed forward. I was on an errand I did not wish to make to talk to a person I had no desire to see about the troubles of an aunt I loathed. To do so I had to spend hours stalled in traffic. And my feet were cold inside their open-toed pumps. I turned up the heat further but the little Omega didn't respond. I curled and uncurled my toes to get the blood moving but they remained obstinately frozen.

At First Avenue the traffic eased up as the offices there sucked up most of the outbound drivers. I exited north at Mannheim and meandered through the streets, trying to follow Albert's roughly sketched directions. It was five after ten when I finally found the priory entrance. Being late did nothing to improve my humor.

The Priory of St. Albertus Magnus included a large block of neo-Gothic buildings set to one side of a beautiful park. The architect apparently believed he had to compensate for the beauties of nature: In the misty snow the gray stone buildings loomed as ungainly shapes.

A small lettered sign identified the nearest concrete block as the House of Studies. As I drove past, a few men in long white robes were scuttling into it, hoods pulled over their faces so that they looked like medieval monks. They paid no attention to me.

As I crept slowly up the circular drive I saw a number of cars parked to one side. I left the Omega there and quickly ran to the nearest entrance. This was labeled simply ST. ALBERT'S PRIORY.

Inside, the building had the half-eerie, half-tired atmosphere you often find in religious institutions. You can tell people spend a lot of time praying there, but perhaps they also spend too much time feeling depressed or bored. The entryway had a vaulted concrete ceiling that disappeared in the gloomy light several stories up. Marble flagstones added to the coldness.

A corridor ran at right angles to the entrance. I crossed to it, my heels echoing in the vaulted chamber, and looked doubtfully around. A scarred wooden desk had been stuck in a corner formed by the entry hall and a stairwell. A thin young man in civvies sat behind it reading *The Greater*

Trumps by Charles Williams. He put it down reluctantly after I'd spoken several times. His face was extremely thin; he seemed to burn with a nervous asceticism, but perhaps he was merely hyperthyroid. At any rate, he directed me to the prior's office in a hurried whisper, not waiting to see if I followed his directions before returning to the book.

At least I was in the right building, a relief since I was now fifteen minutes late. I turned left down the corridor, passing icons and shut doors. A couple of men in white robes passed me, arguing vigorously but in subdued voices. At the end of the hall I turned right. On one side of me was a chapel and across from it, as the youth had promised, the prior's office.

The Reverend Boniface Carroll was on the phone when I came in. He smiled when he saw me and motioned me to a chair in front of his desk, but continued his conversation in a series of grunts. He was a frail man of perhaps fifty. His white woolen robe had turned faintly yellow with age. He looked very tired; as he listened to his caller he kept rubbing his eyes.

The office itself was sparsely furnished. A crucifix over one wall was the only decoration, and the wide desk was scuffed with age. The floor was covered with institutional linoleum, only partly hidden by a threadbare carpet.

"Well, actually she's here right now, Mr. Hatfield. . . . No, no, I think I should talk to her."

I raised my eyebrows at that. The only Hatfield

I knew worked on fraud for the FBI. He was a competent young man, but his sense of humor left something to be desired. When our paths crossed, it was usually to our mutual irritation, since he tried to overcome my flippancy with threats of the might of the FBI.

Carroll terminated the conversation and turned to me. "You are Miss Warshawski, aren't you?" He had a light, pleasant voice with a trace of an eastern accent.

"Yes." I handed him one of my cards. "Was that Derek Hatfield?"

"The FBI man. Yes, he's been out here with Ted Dartmouth from the Securities Exchange Commission. I don't know how he learned we were going to meet, but he was asking me not to talk to you."

"Did he say why?"

"He thinks this is a matter for the FBI and the SEC. He told me an amateur such as yourself might muddy the waters, make the investigation more difficult."

I rubbed my upper lip thoughtfully. I'd forgotten the lipstick until I saw the smear on my forefinger. Cool, Vic. If I were being logical, I'd smile politely at Father Carroll and leave; after all, I'd been cursing him, Rosa, and my mission all the way from Chicago. However, there's nothing like a little opposition to make me change my mind, especially when the opposition comes from Derek Hatfield.

"That's sort of what I said to my aunt when

I talked to her yesterday. The FBI and the SEC are trained to handle this kind of investigation. But she's old and she's scared and she wants someone from the family in her corner.

"I've been a private investigator for almost ten years. I've done a lot of financial crime and I've got a good reputation — I could give you the names of some people in the city to call so you don't have to take just my word for it."

Carroll smiled. "Relax, Miss Warshawski. You don't have to sell me. I told your aunt I would talk to you and I feel we owe her something here, if only a conversation with you. She's worked for St. Albert's very faithfully for a long time. It really hurt her when we asked her to take a leave of absence. I hated doing it, but I've made the same request to everyone with access to the safe. As soon as we get this business cleared up, she knows we want her back. She's extremely competent."

I nodded. I could see Rosa as a competent treasurer. It flashed through my mind that she might have been less angry if she had channeled her energy into a career: She would have made a good corporate financial officer.

"I don't really know what happened," I said to Carroll. "Why don't you tell me the story — where the safe is, how you came to find the fakes, how much money is involved, who could have gotten at them, who knew about them — and I'll butt in when I don't understand."

He smiled again, a shy sweet smile, and got up to show me the safe. It was in a storeroom behind his office, one of those old cast-iron models with a combination lock. It was stuck in a corner amid stacks of paper, an ancient mimeo machine, and piles of extra prayer books.

I knelt to look at it. Of course, the priory had used the same combination for years, which meant anyone who'd been there a while could have found out what it was. Neither the FBI nor the Melrose Park Police had discovered any signs that the lock had been forced.

"How many people do you have here at the priory?"

"There are twenty-one students at the House of Studies and eleven priests on the teaching faculty. But then there are people like your aunt who come in and work during the day. We have a kitchen crew, for example; the brothers do all the washing up and waiting at table, but we have three women who come in to do the cooking. We have two receptionists — the young man who probably directed you to my office and a woman who handles the afternoon shift. And of course there are a lot of neighborhood people who worship with us in the chapel." He smiled again. "We Dominicans are preachers and scholars. We don't usually run parish churches, but a lot of people do treat this as their parish."

I shook my head. "You've got too many people around here to make sorting this out easy. Who actually had official access to the safe?"

"Well, Mrs. Vignelli, of course." That was Rosa. "I do. The procurator — he handles the financial

27

affairs. The student master. We have an audit once a year, and our accountants always examine the stocks, along with the other assets, but I don't think they know the combination to the safe."

"Why'd you keep the things here instead of in a bank vault?"

He shrugged. "I wondered the same thing. I was just elected last May." The smile crept back into his eyes. "Not a post I wanted — I'm like John Roncalli — the safe candidate who doesn't belong to any of the factions here. Anyway, I've never been at all involved in running this — or any other — priory. I didn't know anything about it. I didn't know we kept five million dollars' worth of stock certificates on the premises. To tell you the truth, I didn't even know we owned them."

I shuddered. Five million dollars sitting around for any casual passerby to take. The wonder was that they hadn't simply been stolen years before.

Father Carroll was explaining the history of the stocks in his gentle, efficient voice. They were all blue-chip shares — AT&T, IBM, and Standard of Indiana primarily. They had been left to the priory ten years ago by a wealthy man in Melrose Park.

The priory buildings were close to eighty years old and needed a lot of repairs. He pointed to some cracks in the plaster on the wall and I followed the line of damage to a wide brown stain on the ceiling.

"The most urgent problems are the roof and the furnace. It seemed reasonable to sell some shares and use the money to repair the plant, which is, after all, our main asset. Even though it's ugly and uncomfortable we couldn't begin to replace it today. So I brought up the matter at chapter meeting and got an agreement. The next Monday I went into the Loop and met with a broker. He agreed to sell eighty thousand dollars' worth of shares. He took them from us then."

That had been the last of the matter for a week. Then the broker had called back. The Fort Dearborn Trust, the company's stock-transfer agent, had examined the shares and found they were counterfeits.

"Is there a possibility the broker or the banker made an exchange?"

He shook his head unhappily. "That's the first thing we thought of. But we had all the remaining certificates looked at. They're all fakes."

We sat silently for a bit. What a dispiriting prospect.

"When was the last time the shares were authenticated?" I asked at last.

"I don't know. I called the accountants, but all they do is verify that the shares are there. According to the FBI man, these certificates are extremely good forgeries. They were found out only because the serial numbers had not been used by the issuing companies. They'd fool any ordinary observer."

I sighed. I probably should talk to the former prior, and to the student master and procurator. I asked Carroll about them. His predecessor was in Pakistan for a year, running a Dominican school there. But the student master and procurator were both in the building and would be at lunch.

"You're welcome to join us if you like. Ordinarily the refectory in a convent is cloistered — that means only friars can use the room," he explained in answer to my puzzled look. "And yes. We friars call this a convent. Or a friary. Anyway, we've lifted the cloister here at the school so that the young men can eat with their families when they come to visit. . . . The food isn't very interesting, but it's an easier way to meet Pelly and Jablonski than trying to track them down afterward." He pulled back a yellowed sleeve to reveal a thin wrist with a heavy leather watchband on it. "It's almost noon. People will be gathering outside the refectory now."

I looked at my own watch. It was twenty of twelve. Duty had driven me to worse things than undistinguished cuisine. I accepted. The prior locked the storeroom carefully behind him. "Another example of locking the barn door," he said. "There was no lock on that storeroom until we discovered the fake securities."

We joined a throng of white-robed men walking down the corridor past Carroll's office. Most of them said hello to him, eyeing me covertly. At the end of the hall were two swinging doors. Through their glass top halves I could see the refectory, looking like a high-school gym converted to a lunch room: long deal tables, metal folding chairs, no linens, hospital-green walls.

Carroll took me by the arm and led me through the huddle to a pudgy middle-aged man whose head emerged from a fringe of gray hair, like a soft-boiled egg from an egg cup. "Stephen, I'd like you to meet Miss Warshawski. She's Rosa Vignelli's niece, but she's also a private investigator. She's looking into our crime as an *amica familiae*." He turned to me. "This is Father Jablonski, who's been the student master for seven years. . . . Stephen, why don't you dig up Augustine and introduce him to Miss Warshawski. She needs to talk to him, too."

I was about to murmur a social inanity when Carroll turned to the crowd and said something in Latin. They answered and he rattled off what I assumed was a blessing; everyone crossed himself.

Lunch was definitely uninteresting: bowls of Campbell's tomato soup, which I loathe, and toasted cheese sandwiches. I put pickles and onions inside my sandwich and accepted coffee from an eager young Dominican.

Jablonski introduced me to Augustine Pelly, the procurator, and to some half dozen other men at our table. These were all "brothers," not "fathers." Since they tended to look alike in their fresh white robes I promptly forgot their names.

"Miss Warshawski thinks she can succeed where the FBI and the SEC are baffled," Jablonski said jovially, his nasal midwestern accent blaring above the dining room cacophony.

Pelly gave me a measuring look, then smiled.

31

He was almost as thin as Father Carroll, and very tanned, which surprised me — where did a monk go sunbathing in midwinter? His blue eyes were sharp and alert in his dark face. "I'm sorry, Miss Warshawski — I know Stephen well enough to tell he's joking, but I'm afraid I don't get the joke."

"I'm a private investigator," I explained.

Pelly raised his eyebrows. "And you're going to look into our missing securities?"

I shook my head. "I don't really have the resources to match the FBI on that type of thing. But I'm also Rosa Vignelli's niece; she wants someone from the family on her side in the investigation. A lot of people have had access to that safe over the years; I'm here to remind Derek Hatfield of that if he starts breathing down Rosa's neck too hard."

Pelly smiled again. "Mrs. Vignelli doesn't strike one as the type of woman to need protection."

I grinned back at him. "She certainly doesn't, Father Pelly. But I keep reminding myself that Rosa's been aging just like any other human being. At any rate, she seems a little frightened, especially that she won't be able to work here anymore." I ate some of my sandwich. Kraft American. Next to Stilton and Brie my favorite cheese.

Jablonski said, "I hope she knows that Augustine and I are also forbidden access to the priory's finances until this matter is cleared up. She's not being singled out in any way that we aren't."

"Maybe one of you could call her," I suggested.

"That might make her feel better. . . . I'm sure you know her well enough to realize she's not a woman with a lot of friends. She's centered a good part of her life around this church."

"Yes," Pelly agreed. "I didn't realize she had any family besides her son. She's never mentioned you, Miss Warshawski. Nor that she had any Polish relatives."

"Her brother's daughter was my mother, who married a Chicago policeman named Warshawski. I've never understood the laws of kinship too well. Does that mean that she has Polish relatives because I'm half Polish? You don't think I'm posing as Rosa's niece just to get inside the priory, do you?"

Jablonski gave his sardonic smile. "Now that the securities are gone, there's nothing worth worming your way into the priory for. Unless you have some secret fetish for friars."

I laughed, but Pelly said seriously, "I assume the prior looked into your credentials."

"There wasn't any reason for him to; he wasn't hiring me. I do have a copy of my P.I. license on me, but I don't carry any identification that proves I'm Rosa Vignelli's niece. You could call her, of course."

Pelly held up a hand. "I'm not doubting you. I'm just concerned for the priory. We're getting some publicity which none of us relishes and which is really detrimental to the studies of these young men." He indicated the intently eavesdropping young brothers at our table. One of them blushed

33

in embarrassment. "I really don't want anyone, even if she's the pope's niece, stirring things up here further."

"I can understand that. But I can also see Rosa's point — it's just too convenient to have her on the outside of the priory taking the fall. She doesn't have a big organization with lots of political connections behind her. You do."

Pelly gave me a freezing stare. "I won't attempt to untangle that one, Miss Warshawski. You obviously are referring to the popular myth about the political power of the Catholic Church, the direct line from the Vatican that was going to control John Kennedy, that sort of thing. It's beneath discussion."

"I think we could have a pretty lively discussion about it," I objected. "We could talk about the politics of abortion, for example. How local pastors try to influence their congregations to vote for anti-choice candidates regardless of how terrible their qualifications may be otherwise. Or maybe you'd like to discuss the relations between Archbishop Farber and Police Superintendent Bellamy. Or even between him and the mayor."

Jablonski turned to me. "I think pastors would be gravely lax in their moral duty if they didn't try to oppose abortion in any way possible, even urging their parishioners to vote for pro-life candidates."

I felt the blood rush to my head, but smiled. "We're never going to agree on whether abortion is a moral issue or a private matter between a woman and her physician. But one thing is clear — it is a highly political issue. There are a lot of people scrutinizing the Catholic Church's involvement in this area.

"Now the tax code spells out pretty specifically how clear of politics you have to stay to keep your tax-exempt status. So when bishops and priests are using their offices to push political candidates, they're walking a pretty thin line on tax-exempt status. So far, no tax-court judge has been willing to take on the Catholic Church — which in itself argues some hefty clout."

Pelly turned an angry crimson under his tan. "I don't think you have the least idea what you're talking about, Miss Warshawski. Maybe you could keep your remarks to the specific points that the prior asked you to discuss."

"Fine," I said. "Let's concentrate on the priory here. Is there anyone who would have a reason to take close to five million dollars?"

"No one," Pelly said shortly. "We take vows of poverty." One of the brothers offered me more coffee. It was so thin as to be almost undrinkable, but I accepted it absently.

"You got the shares ten years ago. Since then, almost anyone with access to the priory could have taken the money. Discounting random strangers walking in off the street, that means someone connected with this place. What kind of turnover do you have among your monks?"

"They're actually called friars," Jablonski interjected. "Monks stay in one place; friars roam around. What do you mean by turnover? Every year students leave — some have been ordained, others find the conventual life doesn't suit them for some reason. And there's a lot of movement among the priests, too. People who taught at other Dominican institutions come here, or vice versa. Father Pelly here just returned from six months in Ciudad Isabella. He was a student in Panama and likes to spend a certain amount of time down there."

That explained his suntan, then. "We can probably eliminate people who move on to other Dominican seats. But what about any young men who've left the order in the last decade? Could you find out if any of them claimed coming into an inheritance?"

Pelly shrugged disdainfully. "I suppose so, but I would be most reluctant to do so. When Stephen said young men find the monastic life doesn't suit them, it's not usually because of lack of luxury. We do a careful screening of our applicants before we allow them to become novices. I think we'd turn up the type who would steal."

Father Carroll joined us at that point. The refectory was clearing. Knots of men stood talking in the doorway, some staring at me. The prior turned to the brothers lingering at our table. "Don't you have exams next week? Perhaps you should be studying."

They got up a little shamefacedly and Carroll sat in one of the empty seats. "Are you making any progress?"

Pelly frowned. "We've progressed past some wild accusations about the Church in general to a concentrated attack on young men who have left the order in the last decade. Not exactly what I'd expect from a Catholic girl."

I held up a hand. "Not me, Father Pelly. I'm not a girl and I'm not a Catholic. . . . We're really at a standstill. I'll have to talk to Derek Hatfield and see if he'll share the FBI's ideas with me. What you need to find is someone with a secret bank account. Perhaps one of your brothers, possibly my aunt. Although if she stole the money, it certainly wasn't to use on herself. She lives very frugally. Perhaps, though, she's a fanatic about some cause I don't know anything about and stole to support it. Which might be true of any of you as well."

Rosa as a secret Torquemada appealed to me but there wasn't any real evidence of it. It was hard to imagine her feeling positive enough about anyone or anything to love it, let alone steal for it.

"As the procurator, Father Pelly, perhaps you know whether the shares were ever authenticated. If this wasn't done when you got them, it's possible they came to you as forgeries."

Pelly shook his head. "It never occurred to us. I don't know if we're too unworldly to handle assets, but it doesn't seem like the kind of thing anyone does."

"Probably not," I agreed. I asked him and Jablonski some more questions, but neither was very helpful. Pelly still seemed miffed with me over the Church and politics. Since I'd compounded my sin by not being a Catholic girl, his answers were fairly frosty. Even Jablonski commented on it.

"Why are you on such a high horse with Miss Warshawski, Gus? So she's not a Catholic. Neither is eighty-five percent of the world's population. That should make us more charitable, not less."

Pelly turned his cold stare on him, and Carroll remarked, "Let's save group criticism for chapter, Stephen."

Pelly said, "I'm sorry if I seem rude, Miss Warshawski. But this business is very worrying, especially because I was the procurator for eight years. And I'm afraid my experiences in Central America make me sensitive to criticisms about the Church and politics."

I blinked a few times. "Sensitive how?"

Carroll intervened again. "Two of our priests were shot in El Salvador last spring; the government suspected they were harboring rebels."

I didn't say anything. Whether the Church was working for the poor, as in El Salvador, or supporting the government, as in Spain, it was still, in my book, up to its neck in politics. But it didn't seem polite to pursue the argument.

Jablonski thought otherwise. "Rubbish, Gus, and you know it. You're only upset because you and the government don't see eye to eye. But if your friends have their way, you know very well that the Friars of San Tomás will have some very powerful allies." He turned to me. "That's the trouble with people like you and Gus, Miss Warshawski — when the Church is on your side, whether it's fighting racism or poverty, it's just being sensitive, not political. When it goes against your position, then it's political and up to no good."

Carroll said, "I think we're all getting a long way from Miss Warshawski's real business in coming out here. Stephen, I know we Dominicans are supposed to be preachers, but it violates some rules of hospitality to preach at a guest over lunch, even so meager a lunch as this."

He stood up and the rest of us got up also. As we walked from the refectory, Jablonski said, "No hard feelings, Miss Warshawski. I like a good fighter. Sorry if I offended you in your role as a guest."

To my surprise I found myself smiling at him. "No hard feelings, Father. I'm afraid I got a little carried away myself."

He shook hands with me briskly and walked down the hall in the opposite direction from Carroll, who said, "Good. I'm glad you and Stephen found some common ground. He's a good man, just a little aggressive sometimes."

Pelly frowned. "Aggressive! He's completely without — " He suddenly remembered to save group criticism for chapter and broke off. "Sorry, Prior. Maybe I should go back to San Tomás — that's where my mind seems to be these days."

IV

Return Engagement

It was close to three when I threaded my way to my office in the South Loop. It's in the Pulteney Building, which is of the right vintage to be a national historic landmark. I sometimes think it might even qualify if it ever acquired a management interested in looking after it. Buildings around there don't fare well. They're too close to the city lockup, the slums, the peepshows and the cheap bars, so they attract clients like me: detectives on shoestring budgets, bail bondsmen, inept secretarial services.

I put the car into a lot on Adams and walked the block north to the Pulteney. The snow, or rain, or whatever it was had stopped. While the skies were still sullen, the pavement was almost dry and my beloved Magli pumps were free from further insults.

Someone had left a bourbon bottle in the lobby. I picked it up and carried it with me to throw out in my office. My long-awaited oil-tanker billionaire might show up and be put off by empty whiskey bottles in the lobby. Especially if he saw the brand.

The elevator, working for a change, clanked lugubriously down from the sixteenth floor. I stuck the bottle under one arm and slid open an ancient brass grille with the other. If I never worked out I'd stay in shape just by coming to the office every day — between running the elevator, repairing the toilet in the ladies' room on the seventh floor, and walking up and down the stairs between my fourth-floor office and the bathroom.

The elevator grudgingly stopped at the fourth floor. My office was at the east end of the corridor, the end where low rents sank even further because of the noise of the Dan Ryan L running directly underneath it. A train was clattering by as I unlocked the door.

I spend so little time in my office that I've never put much into furnishing it. The old wooden desk I'd bought at a police auction. That was it, except for two straight-backed chairs for clients, my chair, and an army-green filing cabinet. My one concession to grace was an engraving of the Ufizzi over the filing cabinet.

I picked up a week's accumulation of mail from the floor and started opening it while I called my answering service. Two messages. I didn't need to get in touch with Hatfield; he'd called me and would see me in his office at nine the next morning.

I looked at a bill from a stationery company. Two hundred dollars for letterhead and envelopes? I put it in the trash and dialed the FBI. Hatfield wasn't in, of course. I got his secretary. "Yes, please tell Derek I won't be free tomorrow morning but three tomorrow afternoon will be fine."

She put me on hold while she checked his calendar. I continued through the mail. The Society of Young Women Business Executives urged me to join. Among their many benefits were a group life and health insurance plan. Derek's secretary came back on the line and we dickered, compromising on two-thirty.

My second message was more of a surprise and much more welcome. Roger Ferrant had called. He was an Englishman, a reinsurance broker whom I'd met the previous spring. His London firm had underwritten a ship that blew up in the Great Lakes. I was investigating the disaster; his firm was protecting its fifty-million-dollar investment. We hadn't seen each other since a night when I'd fallen asleep — to put it politely — across from him at a posh steakhouse.

I reached him at his firm's apartment in the Hancock Building. "Roger! What are you doing in Chicago?"

"Hello, Vic. Scupperfield, Plouder sent me over here for a few weeks. Can we have dinner?"

"Is this my second chance? Or did you like my act the first time so well you want an encore?"

He laughed. "Neither. How about it? Are you free this week anytime?"

I told him I was free that very night and agreed to meet him at the Hancock Building for a drink at seven-thirty. I hung up in much better spirits — I deserved a reward for messing around in Rosa's affairs.

I quickly sorted through the rest of my mail.

None of it needed answering. One envelope actually contained a check for three hundred fifty dollars. Way to pick your clients, Vic, I cheered silently. Before leaving, I typed out a few bills on the old Olivetti that had been my mother's. She subscribed firmly to the belief that IBM had stolen both the Executive and Selectric designs from Olivetti and would have been ashamed of me if I'd owned one of the Itsy-Bitsy Machine Company's models.

I quickly finished the bills, stuffed them in envelopes, turned out the lights, and locked up. Outside the street was jammed with rush-hour crowds. I jostled and darted my way through them with the ease of long experience and retrieved the Omega for another long slow drive through stop-and-go traffic.

I bore the delays meekly, swooping off the Kennedy at Belmont and detouring around to my bank with the check before going home. In a sudden burst of energy I washed the dishes before changing clothes. I kept on the yellow silk top, found a pair of black velvet slacks in the closet, and put on a black-and-orange scarf. Eye-catching but not vulgar.

Ferrant seemed to think so, too. He greeted me enthusiastically in the Scupperfield, Plouder apartment at the Hancock. "I remembered you were tough and funny, Vic, but I'd forgotten how attractive you are."

If you like thin men, which I do, Ferrant looked good himself. He had on well-tailored casual slacks with tiny pleats at the waist, and a dark green sweater over a pale yellow shirt. His dark hair, which had been carefully combed when he opened the door, fell into his eyes when I returned his hug. He pushed it back with a characteristic gesture.

I asked what brought him to Chicago.

"Business with Ajax, of course." He led me into the living room, a modernistically furnished square overlooking the lake. A large orange couch with a glass-and-chrome coffee table in front of it was flanked by chrome chairs with black fabric seats. I winced slightly.

"Hideous, isn't it?" he said cheerfully. "If I have to stay in Chicago more than a month, I'm going to make them let me get my own apartment. Or at least my own furniture. . . . Do you drink anything besides Chateau St. Georges? We have a complete liquor cabinet."

He swept open a blond-and-glass cabinet in one corner to display an impressive array of bottles. I laughed: I'd drunk two bottles of Chateau St. Georges when we went to dinner together last May. "Johnny Walker Black if they have it." He rummaged through the cupboard, found a half-used bottle, and poured each of us a modest drink.

"They must hate you in London to send you to Chicago in January. And if you have to stay through February you'll know you're really on their hit list."

He grimaced. "I've been here before in winter. It must explain why you American girls are so

44

tough. Are they as hard-boiled as you in South?"

"Worse," I assured him. "They're tougher but they hide it under this veneer of soft manners, so you don't know you've been hit until you start coming to."

I sat at one end of the orange couch; he pulled up one of the chrome chairs close to me and leaned storklike over his drink, his hair falling into his eyes again. He explained that Scupperfield, Plouder, his London firm, owned three percent of Ajax. "We're not the largest stockholder, but we're an important one. So we keep a finger in the Ajax pie. We send our young fellows here for training and take some Ajax people and teach them the London market. Believe it or not, I was a young fellow once myself." Like many people in English insurance, Ferrant had started to work right after high school, or what we think of as high school. So at thirty-seven he had close to twenty years of experience in the topsy-turvy reinsurance business.

"I'm telling you that so you won't be so startled to hear I'm now a corporate officer *pro tem*." He grinned. "A lot of people at Ajax feel their noses bent because I'm so young, but by the time they have my experience, they'll be six or eight years older."

Aaron Carter, the head of Ajax's reinsurance division, had died suddenly last month of a heart attack. His most likely successor had left in September to join a rival company. "I'm just filling in until they can find someone with the right qual-

45

ifications. They need a good manager, but they must find someone who knows the London market upside down."

He asked me what I was working on. I had a few routine cases going, but nothing interesting, so I told him about my aunt Rosa and the counterfeit securities. "I'd love to see her put away for securities fraud, but I'm afraid she's just an innocent bystander." On second thought, no one who ever met Rosa would think of her as innocent. Crime-free might be a better adjective.

I declined a second scotch, and we put on our coats to go into the winter night. A strong wind was blowing across the lake, driving away the clouds but dropping the temperature down to the teens. We held hands and half ran into its face to an Italian restaurant four blocks away on Seneca.

Despite its location in the convention district, the Caffe Firenze had a cheerful unpretentious interior. "I didn't know you were part Italian when I made the reservation, or I might have hesitated," Ferrant said as we turned our coats over to a plump young girl. "Do you know this place? Is the food authentic?"

"I've never heard of it, but I don't eat in this part of town too often. As long as they make their own pasta we should be fine."

I followed the maître d' to a booth against the far wall. Firenze avoided the red-checked cloth and Chianti bottles so many Italian restaurants display in Chicago. The polished wood table had linen placemats on it and a flower stuck in a Tuscan pottery vase.

We ordered a bottle of Ruffino and some *pasticcini di spinaci,* enchanting the waiter by speaking Italian. It turned out Ferrant had visited the country numerous times and spoke Italian passably well. He asked if I'd ever seen my mother's family there.

I shook my head. "My mother's from Florence, but her family was half Jewish — her mother came from a family of scholars in Pitigliano. They scattered widely at the outbreak of the war — my mother came here, her brother went to Africa, and the cousins went every which way. My grandmother died during the war. Gabriella went back once in 1955 to see her father, but it was depressing. He was the only member of her immediate family left in Florence and she said he couldn't deal with the war or the changes it brought; he kept pretending it was 1936 and the family was still together. I think he's still alive but — " I made a gesture of distaste. "My dad wrote him when my mother died and we got back a very unsettling letter inviting us to hear her sing. I've never felt like dealing with him."

"Was your mother a singer, then?"

"She'd trained as one. She'd hoped to sing opera. Then, when she had to flee the country, she couldn't afford to continue her lessons. She taught instead. She taught me. She hoped I'd pick it up and have her career for her. But I don't have a big enough voice. And I don't really like opera all that well."

Ferrant said apologetically that he always had tickets for the Royal Opera and enjoyed it thoroughly.

I laughed. "I enjoy the staging and the sheer — virtuosity, I guess it is — of putting an opera together. It's very strenuous work, you know. But the singing is too violent. I prefer *Lieder*. My mother always saved enough money from the music lessons to take the two of us to a couple of Lyric Opera performances every fall. Then in the summer my dad would take me to see the Cubs four or five times. The Lyric Opera is better than the Chicago Cubs, but I have to admit I've always gotten more pleasure from baseball."

We ordered dinner — fried artichoke and *pollo in galantina* for me, veal kidneys for Ferrant. The talk moved from baseball to cricket, which Ferrant played, to his own childhood in Highgate, and finally to his career in Scupperfield, Plouder.

As I was finishing my second cup of espresso, he asked me idly if I followed the stock market at all.

I shook my head. "I don't have anything to invest. Why?" He shrugged. "I've only been here a week, but I noticed in *The Wall Street Journal* that Ajax's volume seems quite heavy compared to the other stock-insurance companies, and the price seems to be going up."

"Great. Looks like your firm picked a winner."

He signaled for the check. "We're not doing anything spectacular in the way of earnings. Not buying any companies or selling off any properties. What else makes a share price go up?"

"Sometimes institutional investors take a whimsical fancy to a stock. Insurance companies fared better during the last depression or recession or whatever than most businesses. Ajax is one of the biggest — maybe the funds and the other big investors are just playing it safe. . . . If you want, I could give you the name of a broker I know; she might have some other information."

"Maybe so."

We collected our coats and headed back into the wind. It was blowing harder, but fried artichokes and half a bottle of wine made it seem less penetrating. Ferrant invited me up for a brandy.

He turned the lamp by the bar on a low switch. We could see the bottles but the garish furniture was mercifully muted. I stood at the window looking down at the lake. Ice reflected the streetlights on Lake Shore Drive. By squinting I could make out the promontories farther south, which held Navy Pier and McCormick Place. In the clear winter air the South Works twelve miles away glowed red. I used to live there in an ill-built wooden row house, made distinctive by my mother's artistry.

Ferrant put his left arm around me and handed me a snifter of Martell with the right. I leaned back against him, then turned and put both arms around him, carefully holding the snifter away from his sweater. It felt like cashmere and might not take kindly to brandy. He was thin but wiry, not just an opera-loving beanpole. He slid his hand under my silk top and stroked my back, then began fumbling for the bra strap.

"It opens in front." I was having a hard time maintaining my balance and the snifter at the same time, so I put the brandy down on the window ledge behind me. Ferrant had found the front hook. I fumbled with the buttons on his pleated trousers. Making love standing up is not as easy as they make it look in the movies. We slid down onto the thick orange carpet together.

V

Frustration

We finished the brandy and the rest of the night in a king-sized bed with a blond Scandinavian headboard. When we woke up well after eight the next morning, Ferrant and I smiled at each other with sleepy pleasure. He looked fresh and vulnerable with his dark hair hanging down in his dark blue eyes; I put an arm around him and kissed him.

He kissed me back enthusiastically, then sat up. "America is a country of terrible contrasts. They give you these wonderful outsize beds, which I'd give a month's pay for back home, then they expect you to hop out of them in the middle of the night to be at work. In London I wouldn't dream of being in the City before nine-thirty at the earliest, but here my whole staff has already been at the office for half an hour. I'd better get going."

I lay back in bed and watched him go through the male dressing ritual, which ended when he had encased his neck meekly in a gray-and-burgundy choker. He tossed me a blue paisley robe and I got up to drink a cup of coffee with him, pleased with my foresight in changing my meeting with Hatfield to the afternoon.

After Ferrant left, muttering curses against the

51

American work ethic, I phoned my answering service. My cousin Albert had called three times, once late last night and twice this morning. The second time he'd left his office number. My pleasure in the morning began to evaporate. I put on last night's clothes, frowning at myself in the wide mirrors that served as closet doors. An outfit that looks sexy at night tends to appear tawdry in the morning. I was going to have to change for my meeting with Hatfield; I might as well go home and do it before calling Albert.

I paid dearly for parking the Omega at the Hancock Building for fourteen hours. That did nothing to cheer me up, and I earned a whistle and a yell from the traffic cop at Oak Street for swinging around the turning traffic onto the Lake Shore Drive underpass. I sobered up then. My father had drummed into my head at an early age the stupidity of venting anger with a moving car. He was a policeman and had taken guns and cars very seriously — he spent too much time with the wreckage of those who used such lethal weapons in anger.

I stopped for a breakfast falafel sandwich at a storefront Lebanese restaurant at Halsted and Wrightwood and ate it at the red lights the rest of the way up Halsted. The decimation of Lebanon was showing up in Chicago as a series of restaurants and little shops, just as the destruction of Vietnam had been visible here a decade earlier. If you never read the news but ate out a lot you should be able to tell who was getting beaten up around the world.

From North Avenue to Fullerton, Halsted is part of the recently renovated North Side, where young professionals pay two hundred fifty thousand or more for chic brick townhouses. Four blocks farther north, at Diversey, the rich have not yet stuck out rehabilitation tentacles. Most of the buildings, like mine, are comfortably run-down. One advantage is the cheap rents; the other is space to park on the street.

I stopped the Omega in front of my building and went inside to change back into the navy walking suit for my meeting with Hatfield. By then I had delayed calling Albert long enough. I took a cup of coffee into the living room and sat in the overstuffed armchair while I phoned. I studied my toes through my nylons. Maybe I'd paint the nails red. I can't stand nail polish on my fingers, but it might be sexy on my toes.

A woman answered Albert's work number. His secret lover, I thought: Rosa assumes she's his secretary, but he secretly buys her perfume and *zabiglione.* I asked for Albert; she said in a nasal, uneducated voice that "Mr. Vignelli" was in conference and would I leave a message.

"This is V.I. Warshawski," I said. "He wants to talk to me. Tell him this is the only time I'll be available today."

She put me on hold. I drank coffee and started an article in *Fortune* on chicanery at CitiCorp. I was delighted. I've never forgiven them for taking two years to answer a billing complaint. I was just getting into illegal currency manipulation when Albert came on the line, sounding more petulant than usual.

"Where have *you* been?"

I raised my eyebrows at the mouthpiece. "At an all-night sex and dope orgy. The sex was terrible but the coke was really great. Want to come next time?"

"I might have known you'd just laugh instead of taking Mama's problems seriously."

"I'm not laughing, Albert. If you read the paper, you know how hard it is to get good coke these days. But tell me, has Rosa's problem taken a turn for the worse? Just to show you I mean well, I won't even charge you for my time waiting on hold."

I could visualize his fat round face puckered up in a full-scale pout as he breathed heavily into my ear. At last he said angrily, "You went to St. Albert's Priory yesterday, didn't you?"

I assented.

"What did you find out?"

"That this is going to be incredibly tough to sort out. Our best hope is that the securities had already been faked before the priory got them. I'm meeting with the FBI this afternoon and I'm going to see if they're looking into that."

"Well, Mama has changed her mind. She doesn't want you to investigate this after all."

I sat frozen for a few seconds while anger came to a focus inside my head. "What the hell do you mean, Albert? I'm not a vacuum cleaner that you

54

switch on and off at will. You don't start me on an investigation, then call up two days later to say you've changed your mind."

I could hear paper rustling in the background, then Albert said smugly, "Your contract doesn't say that. It just says 'Termination of the case may be requested by either party, whether the requested results are obtained or not. Regardless of the state of the investigation, and regardless of whether either party disagrees with the results, the fee and expenses incurred to the time of termination shall be paid.' If you send me a bill, Victoria, I'll pay it promptly."

I could smell my brain burning. "Albert. When Rosa called me on Sunday she made it sound as though her suicide would be on my head if I didn't come out and help her. What's happened since then? She find a detective she likes better? Or did Carroll call and promise her her job back if she'd get me out of the investigation?"

He said aloofly, "She told me last night she felt she was acting in a very unchristian way by getting so worried about this. She knows her name will be cleared; if it's not, she'll bear it like a Christian."

"How noble," I said sarcastically. "Rosa as a bitter martyr is a pose I know well. But the woman of sorrows is a new departure."

"Really, Victoria. You're acting like an ambulance chaser. Just send me a bill."

At least I had the dubious satisfaction of hanging up first. I sat fuming, cursing Rosa in Italian, then

55

in English. Just like her to jack me around! Get me out to Melrose Park by screaming about Gabriella and my duty to my dead mother, if not to my live aunt, send me off on a wild-goose chase, then call the whole thing off. I was strongly tempted to phone her and tell her once and for all exactly what I thought of her, omitting no detail, however slight. I even looked her number up in my address book and started dialing before I realized the futility of such an act. Rosa was seventy-five. She was not going to change. If I couldn't accept that, then I was doomed to be a victim of her manipulation forever.

I sat for a while with *Fortune* open in my lap, staring across the room at the gray day outside. Last night's strong wind had blown clouds in front of it across the lake. What was Rosa's real reason for wanting the investigation to stop? She was cold, angry, vindictive — a dozen disagreeable adjectives. But not a schemer. She wouldn't call a hated niece after a ten-year hiatus just to run me through hoops.

I looked up St. Albert's Priory in the phone book and called Carroll. The call went through a switchboard. I could see the ascetic young man at the reception desk reluctantly putting down his Charles Williams to answer the phone on the sixth ring, picking up the book again before switching the call through. I waited several minutes for the prior. At last Carroll's educated, gentle voice came on the line.

"This is V.I. Warshawski, Father Carroll."

He apologized for keeping me waiting; he'd been going over the household accounts with the head cook and the receptionist had paged the kitchen last.

"No problem," I said. "I wondered if you'd spoken with my aunt since I saw you yesterday."

"With Mrs. Vignelli? No. Why?"

"She's decided suddenly that she doesn't want any investigation into the counterfeit securities, at least not on her behalf. She seems to think that worrying about them is very unchristian. I wondered if someone at the priory had been counseling her."

"Unchristian? What a curious idea. I don't know; I suppose it would be if she got absorbed by this problem to the exclusion of other more fundamental matters. But it's very human to worry about a fraud that might harm your reputation. And if you think of being Christian as a way to be more fully human, it would be a mistake to make someone feel guilty for having natural human feelings."

I blinked a few times. "So you didn't tell my aunt to drop the investigation?"

He gave a soft laugh. "You didn't want me to build a watch; you just wanted the time. No, I haven't talked to your aunt. But it sounds as though I should."

"And did anyone else at the priory? Talk to her, I mean." Not as far as he knew, but he'd ask around and get back to me. He wanted to know if I had learned anything useful yet. I told him

57

I'd be talking to Hatfield that afternoon, and we hung up with mutual promises to stay in touch.

I puttered around the apartment, hanging up clothes and putting a week's accumulation of newspapers into a stack on the back porch where my landlord's grandson would collect them for recycling. I made myself a salad with cubes of cheddar cheese in it and ate it while flicking aimlessly through yesterday's *Wall Street Journal*. At twelve-thirty I went down for the mail.

When you thought about it seriously, Rosa was an old lady. She probably had imagined she could make her problem disappear by scowling at it, the way she'd made all her problems, including her husband, Carl, disappear. She thought if she called me and ordered me to take care of it, it would go away. When the reality came a little closer after she'd talked with me, she decided it just wasn't worth the energy it would take to fight it. My problem was that I was so wound up in all the old enmities that I suspected everything she did was motivated by hatred and a need for revenge.

Ferrant called at one, partly for some light chat, and partly because of questions about Ajax's stock. "One of my responsibilities seems to be our investment division. So I got a call today from a chap named Barrett in New York. He called himself the Ajax specialist at the New York Stock Exchange. I know reinsurance, not the U.S. stock market, or even the London stock market, so I had some trouble keeping up with him. But you remember I told you last night our stock seemed

58

really active? Barrett called to tell me that. Called to let me know he was getting a lot of orders from a small group of Chicago brokers who had never traded in Ajax before. Nothing wrong with them, you understand, but he thought I should know about it."

"And?"

"Now I know about it. But I'm not sure what, if anything, I should do. So I'd like to meet that friend you mentioned — the one who's the broker."

Agnes Paciorek and I had met at the University of Chicago when I was in law school and she was a math whiz turned MBA. We actually met at sessions of University Women United. She was a maverick in the gray-tailored world of MBAs and we'd remained good friends.

I gave Roger her number. After hanging up I looked up Ajax in *The Wall Street Journal*. Their range for the year went from 28¼ to 55½ and they were currently trading at their high. Aetna and Cigna, the two largest stock-insurance carriers, had similar bottom prices, but their highs were about ten points below Ajax. Yesterday they'd each had a volume of about three hundred thousand, compared to Ajax's, which was almost a million. Interesting.

I thought about calling Agnes myself, but it was getting close to time for me to leave to meet Hatfield. I wrapped a mohair scarf around my neck, pulled on some driving gloves, and went back out into the wind. Two o'clock is a good time to drive into the Loop. The traffic is light. I made it to the Federal Building on Dearborn and Adams in good time, left the Omega in a self-park garage across the street and walked in under the orange legs of the three-story Calder designed for Chicago's Federal Building. We pride ourselves in Chicago on our outdoor sculptures by famous artists. My favorite is the bronze wind chimes in front of the Standard Oil Building, but I have a secret fondness for Chagall's mosaics in front of the First National Bank. My artist friends tell me they are banal.

It was exactly two-thirty when I reached the FBI offices on the eighteenth floor. The receptionist phoned my name in to Hatfield, but he had to keep me waiting ten minutes just to impress me with how heavily Chicago's crime rested on his shoulders. I busied myself with a report for a client whose brother-in-law had been pilfering supplies, apparently out of bitterness from some longstanding family feud. When Hatfield finally stuck his head around the corner from the hall, I affected not to hear him until the second time he called my name. I looked up then and smiled and said I would be just a minute and carefully finished writing a sentence.

"Hello, Derek," I said. "How's crime?"

For some reason this jolly greeting always makes him grimace, which is probably why I always use it. His face has the bland handsomeness required by the FBI. He's around six feet tall with a square build. I could see him doing a hundred sit-ups and push-ups every morning with methodical un-complaining discipline, always turning down the second martini, picking up only college girls to make sure someone with a modicum of brains would breathe in his ear how smart and how brave he was. He was dressed today in a gray-plaid suit — muted gray on slightly paler gray with the discreetest of blue stripes woven in — a white shirt whose starch could probably hold up my brassiere for a week, and a blue tie.

"I don't have a lot of time, Warshawski." He shot back a starched cuff and looked at his watch. Probably a Rolex.

"I'm flattered, then, that you wanted to make some of it available to me." I followed him down the hall to an office in the southwestern corner. Hatfield was head of white-collar crime for the Chicago Region, obviously a substantial position judging by the furniture — all wood veneer — and the location.

"That's a nice view of the metropolitan lockup," I said, looking out at the triangular building. "It must be a great inspiration for you."

"We don't send anyone there."

"Not even for overnight holding? What about Joey Lombardo and Allen Dorfmann? I thought that's where they were staying while they were on trial."

"Could you cut it out? I don't know anything about Dorfmann or Lombardo. I want to talk to you about the securities at St. Albert's."

"Great." I sat down in an uncomfortable chair

covered in tan Naugahyde and put a look of bright interest on my face. "One of the things that occurred to me yesterday was that the certificates might have been forged before they were passed on to St. Albert's. What do you know about the donor and his executors? Also, it is possible some ex-Dominican with a grudge could have been behind it. Do you have a trail on people who left the order in the last ten years?"

"I'm not interested in discussing the case with you, Warshawski. We're very well able to think of leads and follow them up. We have an excellent record here in the bureau. This forgery is a federal offense and I must request you to back out of it."

I leaned forward in my chair. "Derek, I'm not only willing but eager for you to solve this crime. It will take a cast of thousands to sort out. You have that. I don't. I'm just here to make sure that a seventy-five-year-old woman doesn't get crushed by the crowd. And I'd like to know what you've turned up on the possibilities I just mentioned to you."

"We're following all leads."

We argued it back and forth for several more minutes, but he was adamant and I left empty-handed. I stopped in the plaza at a pay phone next to the praying mantis and dialed the *Herald-Star*. Murray Ryerson, their chief crime reporter, was in. He and I have been friends, sometimes lovers, and easy rivals on the crime scene for years.

"Hi, Murray. It's V.I. Is three o'clock too early for a drink?"

"That's no question for the crime desk. I'll connect you with our etiquette specialist." He paused. "A.M. or P.M.?"

"Now, wiseass. I'll buy."

"Gosh, Vic, you must be desperate. Can't do it now, but how about meeting at the Golden Glow in an hour?"

I agreed and hung up. The Golden Glow is my favorite bar in Chicago; I introduced Murray to it a number of years ago. It's tucked away in the DuSable Building, an 1890s skyscraper on Federal, and has the original mahogany bar that Cyrus McCormick and Judge Gary probably used to lean over.

I went to my office to check mail and messages and at four walked back up the street to the bar. Sal, the magnificent black bartender who could teach the Chicago police a thing or two about crowd control, greeted me with a smile and a majestic wave. She wore her hair in an Afro today and had on gold hoop earrings that hung to her shoulders. A shiny blue evening gown showed her splendid cleavage and five-foot eleven frame to advantage. She brought a double Black Label to my corner booth and chatted for a few minutes before getting back to the swelling group of early commuters.

Murray came in a few minutes later, his red hair more disheveled than usual from the January wind. He had on a sheepskin coat and western boots: the urban cowboy. I said as much by way of greeting while a waitress took his order for beer;

Sal only looks after her regular customers personally.

We talked about the poor showing the Black Hawks were making, and about the Greylord trial, and whether Mayor Washington would ever subdue Eddie Vrdolyak. "If Washington didn't have Vrdolyak he'd have to invent him," Murray said. "He's the perfect excuse for Washington not being able to accomplish anything."

The waitress came over. I declined a refill and asked for a glass of water.

Murray ordered a second Beck's. "So what gives, V.I.? I won't say it always spells trouble when you call up out of the blue, but it usually means I end up being used."

"Murray, I bet you a week of my pay that you've gotten more stories out of me than I have gotten clients out of you."

"A week of your pay wouldn't keep me in beer. What's up?"

"Did you pick up a story last week about some forged securities in Melrose Park? Out in a Dominican priory there?"

"Dominican priory?" Murray echoed. "Since when have you started hanging around churches?"

"It's a family obligation," I said with dignity. "You may not know it, but I'm half Italian, and we Italians stick together, through thick and thin. You know, the secret romance of the Mafia and all that. When one member of the family is in trouble, the others rally around."

Murray wasn't impressed. "You going to knock

off somebody in the priory for the sake of your family honor?"

"No, but I might take out Derek Hatfield in the cause."

Murray supported me enthusiastically. Hatfield was as uncooperative with the press as he was with private investigators.

Murray had missed the story of the faked certificates. "Maybe it wasn't on the wires. The feds can be pretty secretive about these things — especially Derek. Think this prior would make a good interview? Maybe I'll send out one of my babies to talk to him."

I suggested he send someone to interview Rosa, and gave him the list of possibilities I'd offered Hatfield. Murray would work those into the story. He'd probably get someone to dig up the name of the original donor and get some public exposure on his heirs. That would force Hatfield to do something — either eliminate them as being involved or publicly announce how old the dud certificates were. "Them that eat cakes that the Parsee man bakes make dreadful mistakes," I muttered to myself.

"What was that?" Murray said sharply. "Are you setting me up to do your dirty work for you, Warshawski?"

I gave him a look that I hoped implied limpid innocence. "Murray! How you talk. I just want to make sure the FBI doesn't railroad my poor frail old aunt." I signaled to Sal that we were ready to leave; she runs a tab that she sends me once a month, the only bill I ever pay on time.

Murray and I moved up north for seafood at the Red Tide. For eight dollars you can get a terrific whole Dungeness crab, which you eat sitting at a bar in a dark basement about half the size of my living room. Afterward I dropped Murray at the Fullerton L stop and went on home alone. I'm past the age where bed-hopping has much appeal.

VI

Uncle Stefan's Profession

Snow was falling the next morning as I made my five-mile run to Belmont Harbor and back. The ice-filled water was perfectly still. Across the breakwater I could see the lake motionless, too. Not peaceful, but sullenly quiet, its angry gods held tightly by bands of cold.

A Salvation Army volunteer was stamping his feet and calling cheery greetings to commuters at the corner of Belmont and Sheridan. He gave me a smiling "God bless you" as I jogged past. Must be nice to have everything so simple and peaceful. What would he do with an Aunt Rosa? Was there any smile broad enough to make her smile back?

I stopped at a little bakery on Broadway for a cup of cappuccino and a croissant. As I ate at one of the spindly legged tables, I pondered my next actions. I'd met with Hatfield yesterday more out of bravado than anything else — it brought me some sort of perverse pleasure to irritate his well-pressed Brooks Brothers facade. But he wasn't going to do anything for me. I didn't have the resources to pry into the Dominicans. Anyway, even if Murray Ryerson turned something up, what would I do about it if Rosa didn't want me investigating? Wasn't my obligation finished with her abrupt command to stop?

I realized that I was carrying on this internal monologue as an argument with Gabriella, who didn't seem pleased with me for bugging out so early. "Goddamn it, Gabriella," I swore silently. "Why did you make me give you that crazy promise? She hated you. Why do I have to do anything for her?"

If my mother were alive she would shrivel me on the spot for swearing at her. And then turn fierce intelligent eyes on me: So Rosa fired you? Did you go to work only because she hired you?

I slowly finished my cappuccino and went back out into a minor blizzard. Strictly speaking, Rosa had not fired me. Albert had called to say she didn't want me on the job any longer. But was that Albert or Rosa speaking? I should at least get that much clear before deciding what else to do. Which meant another trip to Melrose Park. Not today — the roads would be impossible with the snow: traffic creeping, people falling into ditches. But tomorrow would be Saturday. Even if the weather continued bad there wouldn't be much traffic.

At home I peeled off layers of shirts and leggings and soaked in a hot tub for a while. Being self-employed, I can hold my review of operations and management anywhere. This means time spent thinking in the bath is time spent working. Unfortunately, my accountant doesn't agree that this makes my water bill and bath salts tax deductible.

My theory of detection resembles Julia Child's

approach to cooking: Grab a lot of ingredients from the shelves, put them in a pot and stir, and see what happens. I'd stirred at the priory, and at the FBI. Maybe it was time to let things simmer a bit and see if the smell of cooking gave me any new ideas.

I put on a wool crepe-de-chine pantsuit with a high-necked red-striped blouse and low-heeled black boots. That should be warm enough to walk in if I got stuck in the snow someplace. Wrapping my big mohair scarf around my head and neck, I went back into the storm, adding the Omega to the queue of slowly moving, sliding cars trying to get onto Lake Shore Drive at Belmont.

I crept downtown, barely able to see the cars immediately next to me, and slithered off at Jackson. Leaving the Omega next to a snowdrift behind the Art Institute, I trudged the six blocks to the Pulteney Building, which looked worse than usual in the winter weather. Tenants had tracked snow and mud into the lobby. Tom Czarnik, the angry old man who calls himself the building superintendent, refuses to mop the floor on stormy mornings. His theory is that it will just get nasty again at lunch, so why bother? I should applaud a man whose housekeeping views coincide so closely with mine, but I cursed him under my breath as my boots slid in the lobby slush. The elevator wasn't working today either, so I stomped up four flights of stairs to my office.

After turning on the lights and picking up the mail from the floor, I phoned Agnes Paciorek at her broker's office. On hold while she sold a million shares of AT&T, I looked through bills and pleas for charity. Nothing that wouldn't wait until next month. At last her brisk deep voice came on the line.

"Agnes. It's V.I. Warshawski."

We exchanged pleasantries for a few minutes, then I explained who Roger Ferrant was and said I'd given him her number.

"I know. He called yesterday afternoon. We're meeting for lunch at the Mercantile Club. Are you downtown? Want to join us?"

"Sure. Great. You find anything unusual?"

"Depends on your definition. Brokers don't think buying and selling stock is unusual but you might. I've got to run. See you at one."

The Mercantile Club sits on top of the old Bletchley Iron Building down in the financial district. It's a businessmen's club, which reluctantly opened its doors to women when Mrs. Gray became president of the University of Chicago, since most of the trustees' meetings were held there. Having admitted one woman they found others sneaking through in her wake. The food is excellent and the service impeccable, although some of the old waiters refuse to work tables with women guests.

Ferrant was already sitting by the fire in the reading room where the maître d' sent me to wait for Agnes. He looked elegant in navy-blue tailoring and stood up with a warm smile when he saw me come into the room.

"Agnes invited me to gate-crash; I hope you don't object."

"By no means. You look very smart today. How are your forgeries coming?"

I told him about my useless interview with Hatfield. "And the Dominicans don't know anything, either. At least not about forgery. I need to start at the other end — who could have created them to begin with?"

Agnes came up behind me. "Created what?" She turned to Ferrant and introduced herself, a short, compact dynamo in a brown-plaid suit whose perfect stitching probably required an eight-hundred-dollar investment. Half a day's work for Agnes.

She shepherded us into the dining room where the maître d' greeted her by name and seated us by a window. We looked down at the South Branch of the Chicago River and ordered drinks. I seldom drink whiskey in the middle of the day and asked for oloroso sherry. Ferrant ordered a beer, while Agnes had Perrier with lime — the exchanges didn't close for almost two hours and she believes sober brokers trade better.

Once we were settled she repeated her initial question. I told her about the forgery. "As far as I know, the Fort Dearborn Trust discovered it because the serial numbers hadn't been issued yet. The FBI is being stuffy and close-mouthed, but I know the forgery was pretty high quality — good enough to pass a superficial test by the auditors, anyway. I'd like to talk to someone who knows

71

something about forging — try to find out who'd have the skill to create that good a product."

Agnes cocked a thick eyebrow. "Are you asking me? I just sell 'em; I don't print 'em. Roger's problem is the type of thing I'm equipped to handle. Maybe." She turned to Ferrant. "Why don't you tell me what you know at this point?"

He shrugged thin shoulders. "I told you on the phone about the call from our specialist in New York, Andy Barrett. Maybe you can start by telling me what a specialist is. He doesn't work for Ajax, I take it."

"No. Specialists are members of the New York Stock Exchange — but they're not brokers for the public. Usually they're members of a firm who get a franchise from the Exchange to be specialists — people who manage buy-and-sell orders so business keeps flowing. Barrett makes markets in your stock. Someone wants to sell a thousand shares of Ajax. They call me. I don't go down to the floor of the Chicago Exchange waving 'em around until a buyer happens along — I phone our broker in New York and he goes to Barrett's post on the floor. Barrett buys the shares and makes a match with someone who's looking for a thousand shares. If too many people are unloading Ajax at once and no one wants to buy it, he buys on his own account — he's got an ethical obligation to make markets. Once in a great while, if the market gets completely haywire, he'll ask the Exchange to halt trading in the stock until things shake out."

She paused to give us time to order, Dover sole

for me, rare steaks for her and Roger. She lit a cigarette and began punctuating her comments with stabs of smoke.

"From what I gather, something of the opposite kind has been going on with Ajax the last few weeks. There's been a tremendous amount of buying. About seven times the normal volume, enough that the price is starting to go up. Not a lot — insurance companies aren't glamour investments, so you can have heavy action without too much notice being taken. Did Barrett give you the names of the brokers placing the orders?"

"Yes. They didn't mean anything to me. He's sending a list in the mail. . . . I wondered, if it wouldn't be too great an imposition, Miss Paciorek, whether you'd look at the names when I get them. See if they tell you anything. Also, what should I do?"

To my annoyance, Agnes lit a second cigarette. "No, no imposition. And please call me Agnes. Miss Paciorek sounds too much like the North Shore. . . . I guess what we're assuming, to put the evil thought into blunt words, is that someone may be trying a covert takeover bid. If that's true, they can't have got too far — anyone with five percent or more of the stock has to file with the SEC and explain what's he doing with it. Or she." She grinned at me.

"How much stock would someone need to take over Ajax?" I asked. The food arrived, and Agnes mercifully stubbed out her cigarette.

"Depends. Who besides your firm owns sizable

chunks?" Ferrant shook his head. "I don't really know. Gordon Firth, the chairman. Some of the directors. We own three percent and Edelweiss, the Swiss reinsurers, holds four percent. I think they're the largest owners. Firth maybe owns two. Some of the other directors may have one or two percent."

"So your present management owns around fifteen percent. Someone could carry a lot of weight with sixteen percent. Not guaranteed, but that would be a good place to start, especially if your management wasn't aware it was happening."

I did some mental arithmetic. Fifty million shares outstanding. Sixteen percent would be eight million. "You'd need about five hundred million for a takeover, then."

She thought for a minute. "That's about right. But keep in mind that you don't need to come up with that much capital. Once you've bought a large bloc you can leverage the rest — put your existing shares up as collateral for a loan to buy more shares. Then you leverage those and keep going. Before you know it, you've bought yourself a company. That's oversimplified, of course, but that's the basic idea."

We ate in silence for a minute; then Ferrant said, "What can I do to find out for sure?"

Agnes pursed her square face as she thought about it. "You could call the SEC and ask for a formal investigation. Then you'd be sure of getting the names of the people who are really doing the buying. That's an extreme step, though. Once

74

they're called in they're going to scrutinize every transaction and every broker. You'd want to talk to your board before you did that — some of your directors might not relish having all their stock transactions revealed to the piercing light of day."

"Well, short of that?"

"Every brokerage firm has what we call a compliance officer. Once you get the list of firms from Barrett, you can try calling them and find out on whose behalf they're trading. There's no reason for them to tell you, though — and nothing illegal about trying to buy a company."

The waiters hovered around our table. Dessert? Coffee? Ferrant absentmindedly selected a piece of apple pie. "Do you think they'd talk to you, Miss — Agnes? The compliance officers, I mean. As I told Vic, I'm way out of my depth with this stock-market stuff. Even if you coached me in what to ask, I wouldn't know if the answers I was getting were right."

Agnes put three lumps of sugar in her coffee and stirred vigorously. "It would be unusual. Let me see the list of brokers before I let you know one way or another. What you could do is call Barrett and ask him to send you a list of the names the shares were registered in when he sold them. If I know anyone really well — either the brokers or the customers — I could probably call them."

She looked at her watch. "I've got to get back to the office." She signaled for a waiter and signed the bill. "You two stay though."

Ferrant shook his head. "I'd better call London.

75

It's after eight there — my managing director should be home."

I left with them. The snow had stopped. The sky was clear and the temperature falling. One of the bank thermometers showed 11 degrees. I walked with Roger as far as Ajax. As we said good-bye he invited me to go to a movie with him Saturday night. I accepted, then went on down Wabash to my office to finish the report on pilfered supplies.

During the slow drive home that night, I pondered how to find someone who knew about forging securities. Forgers were engravers gone wrong. And I did know one engraver. At least I knew someone who knew an engraver.

Dr. Charlotte Herschel, Lotty to me, had been born in Vienna, grew up in London where she ultimately received her doctor of medicine degree from London University — and lived about a mile from me on Sheffield Avenue. Her father's brother Stefan, an engraver, had immigrated to Chicago in the twenties. When Lotty decided to come to the States in 1959, she picked Chicago partly because her uncle Stefan lived here. I had never met him — she saw little of him, just saying it made her feel more rooted to have a relative in the area.

My friendship with Lotty goes back a long way, to my student days at the University of Chicago when she was one of the physicians working with an abortion underground I was involved in. She knew Agnes Paciorek from that time, too.

76

I stopped at a Treasure Island on Broadway for groceries and wine. It was six-thirty when I got home and phoned Lotty. She had just come in herself from a long day at the clinic she runs on Sheffield near her apartment. She greeted my offer of dinner enthusiastically and said she would be over after a hot bath.

I cleaned up the worst ravages in my living room and kitchen. Lotty never criticizes my housekeeping, but she is scrupulously tidy herself and it didn't seem fair to drag her out for a brain-picking session on such a cold night, then have her spend it in squalor.

Chicken, garlic, mushrooms, and onions sauteed in olive oil, then flamed with brandy made an easy attractive stew. A cup of Ruffino finished the dish. By the time I had water hot for fettuccine, the doorbell rang.

Lotty came up the stairs briskly and greeted me with a hug. "A lifesaver that you called, my dear. It was a long, very depressing day: a child dead of meningitis because the mother would not bring her in. She hung an amulet around her neck and thought it would bring down a fever of one hundred and four degrees. There are three sisters; we put them in St. Vincent's for observation, but my God!"

I held her for a minute before we went into the apartment, asking if she wanted a drink. Lotty reminded me that alcohol is poison. For extreme situations she believes brandy is permissible, but she did not consider today's woes extreme. I poured myself a glass of Ruffino and put on water for her coffee.

We ate by candlelight in the dining room while Lotty unburdened herself. By the time we had finished the salad, she felt more relaxed and asked me what I was working on.

I told her about Rosa and the Dominicans and Albert's phoning me to tell me the whole thing was off.

The candlelight was reflected in her black eyes as she narrowed them at me. "And what are you trying to prove by continuing?"

"It was Albert who phoned. Rosa may not agree," I said defensively.

"Yes. Your aunt dislikes you. She's decided — for whatever reason — to discontinue the effort to protect herself. So what are you doing? Proving that you are tougher, or smarter, or just plain better than she is?"

I thought it over. Lotty is sometimes about as pleasant as a can opener, but she braces me. I know myself better when I talk to Lotty.

"You know, I don't spend a lot of time thinking about Rosa. It's not as though she's an obsession; she doesn't control my head that much. But I feel very protective of my mother. Rosa hurt her and that makes me angry. If I can show Rosa she was wrong to stop the investigation, that I can solve this problem despite failure by the FBI and the SEC, I'll have proof that she was wrong about everything. And she'll have to believe it." I laughed and finished my glass of wine. "She won't, of course. My rational self knows that. But my feeling self thinks otherwise."

Lotty nodded. "Perfectly logical. Does your rational self have any way of solving this problem?"

"There are lots of things the FBI can do that I can't because they have so much manpower. But one thing I could look into is who actually did the forgeries. Let Derek concentrate on who planted them and which ex-Dominicans are living in luxury.

"I don't know any forgers. But it occurred to me that a forger is really a species of engraver. And I wondered about your uncle Stefan."

Lotty had been watching me with an expression of shrewd amusement. Now her face changed suddenly. Her mouth set and her black eyes narrowed. "Is this an inspired guess? Or have you spent your spare time investigating me?"

I looked at her in bewilderment.

"You wondered why you never met my uncle Stefan? Although he is my only relative living in Chicago?"

"No," I said doggedly. "I never thought about it for a minute. You've never met my aunt Rosa. Even if she weren't a virago, you'd probably never have met her — friends seldom have much in common with relatives."

She continued to stare searchingly at me. I felt very hurt but could think of nothing to say that would bridge the gulf of Lotty's suspicious silence. The last time I had felt this way was the night I realized the man I had married and thought

I loved was as foreign to me as Yasir Arafat. Could a friendship evaporate in the same mist as a marriage?

My throat felt tight, but I forced myself to talk. "Lotty. You've known me for close to twenty years and I've never done anything behind your back. If you think I've started now . . ." That sentence wasn't going in the right direction. "There's something you don't want me to know about your uncle. You don't have to tell me. Carry it to the grave with you. But don't act as though everything you know about me suddenly has no foundation." A light bulb went on over my head. "Oh, no. Don't tell me your uncle really is a forger?"

The set look held in Lotty's face for a few seconds, then cracked into a wry smile. "You are right, Vic. About my uncle. And about you and me. I'm truly sorry, my dear. I won't try to make excuses — there are none. But Stefan . . . When the war ended, I found there was left of my family only my brother and the distant cousins who had taken us in during the war. Hugo — my brother — and I spent what time and money we had searching for relatives. And we found Papa's brother Stefan. When Hugo decided to move to Montreal, I came to Chicago — I had an opportunity for a surgical residency at Northwestern, too good a chance to turn down." She made a throwaway gesture with her left hand. "So I set out to find Uncle Stefan. And discovered him in a federal prison at Fort Leavenworth. Currency was his specialty, although he had a social con-

80

science: He was also forging passports for sale to the many Europeans trying to come to America at the time."

She grinned at me, the old Lotty grin. I leaned across the table and squeezed her hand. She returned the pressure, but went on talking. Detectives and doctors both know the value of talking. "I went to see him. He's likable. Like my father, but without the moral foundation. And I let him stay with me for six months when he was released — 1959 that was; I was his only family, too.

"He got a job, doing custom work for a jeweler — after all, he wasn't a robber, so they weren't afraid he'd lift the sterling. As far as I know, he's never stepped over the edge again. But naturally I haven't asked."

"Naturally not. Well, I will try to find a different engraver."

Lotty smiled again. "Oh, no. Why not call him? He's eighty-two, but he still has all his wits and some besides. He might be the one person who could help you."

She would talk to him the next day and arrange a time when I could have tea with him. We had coffee and pears in the living room and played Scrabble. As usual, Lotty won.

VII

Christian Charity

The air was clear and cold the next morning and a bright winter sun cast a strong glare back from the drifts lining the roads. Halsted had not been plowed, at least not north of Belmont, and the Omega jumped skittishly from rut to rut on the way to the Kennedy Expressway and Melrose Park.

I put on sunglasses and turned on WFMT. Satie. Unbearable. I turned it off again and started singing myself — nothing very noble, just the theme from *Big John and Sparky.* "If you go down to the woods today you'd better not go alone."

It was a little after ten when I turned north on Mannheim and made my way to Rosa's. In Melrose Park, even the side streets had been carefully cleaned. Maybe there was something to be said for suburban living after all. The path leading to her side door had been shoveled neatly, not just a path half a person wide like my building super believed in. There was even something to be said for living with Albert. Which just went to show.

Albert came to the door. The light was behind me and I could see his petulant face through the thick screen. He was surprised and angry. "What are you doing here?"

"Albert. If Rosa has stressed it once, she's stressed a hundred times the importance of families sticking together. I'm sure she'd be shocked to hear you greet me so ungraciously."

"Mama doesn't want to talk to you. I thought I made that clear the other day."

I pulled the screen door open. "Nope. You made it clear you didn't want *me* talking to *her*. That's by no means the same thing."

Albert probably outweighs me by eighty pounds, which may be why he thought it would be easy to push me back out the door. I twisted his left arm up behind him and circled around past him. I hadn't felt so good in weeks.

Rosa's harsh voice wafted down the dim hall from the kitchen, demanding to know who was at the door and why Albert didn't shut it. Didn't he know what they were paying to heat this house?

I followed the voice, Albert walking sulkily behind me. "It's me, Rosa," I said, walking into the kitchen. "I thought we ought to have a little talk about theology."

Rosa was chopping vegetables, presumably for soup, since a shinbone was browning in oil on the stove. The kitchen still had its old 1930s sink. The stove and refrigerator were old, too, small white appliances set against unpainted walls. Rosa put the paring knife down on the counter with a snap, turned full face, and hissed angrily, "I have no wish to talk to you, Victoria!"

I pulled a kitchen chair around and sat backward on it, leaning my chin on its back. "Not good

83

enough, Rosa. I'm not a television that you turn on and off at whim. A week ago you called me and played a tremolo passage on the family violin and dragged me out here against my will. On Thursday, suddenly your morals or ethics got the better of you. You looked at the lilies of the field and decided that it was wrong to have me toiling and spinning over your innocence." I looked at her earnestly. "Rosa, it sounds beautiful. It just doesn't sound like you."

She drew her thin mouth into a tight line. "How should you know? You were never even baptized. I would not expect you to know how a Christian behaves."

"Well, you could be right. The modern world offers few opportunities to see one in action. But you don't understand. You tugged hard on my emotions to get me out here. It's going to be even harder to get rid of me. If you had picked a private investigator out of the Yellow Pages, one who had no connection with you, it would be different. But you insisted on me and it's me you've got."

Rosa sat down. Her eyes blazed fiercely. "I have changed my mind. That is my right. You should not do anything more."

"I want to know something, Rosa. Was this your own idea? Or did someone else suggest it to you?"

Her eyes darted around the kitchen before she spoke. "Naturally I discussed it with Albert."

"Naturally. Your right-hand man and *confidant*. But who else?"

"No one!"

"No, Rosa. That little pause and the look around the room says the opposite. It wasn't Father Carroll, unless he lied to me on Thursday. Who was it?"

She said nothing.

"Who are you protecting, Rosa? Is it someone who knows about these forgeries?"

Still silence.

"I see. You know, the other day I was trying to figure an approach that I was better equipped to handle than the FBI. I came up with one, but you've just offered me a better. I'll get some surveillance on you and find out just who you talk to."

The hate in her face made me recoil physically. "So! What I should have expected from the daughter of a whore!"

Without thinking I leaned forward and slapped her on the mouth. Slyness joined the hate in her face, but she was too proud to rub her mouth where I'd hit it. "You would not love her so much if you knew the truth."

"Thanks, Rosa. I'll be back next week for another lesson in Christian conduct."

Albert had stood silently in the kitchen doorway throughout our altercation. He walked me to the outer door. The smell of burning olive oil followed us down the hall. "You really should knock it off, Victoria. She's pretty worried."

"Why do you stick up for her, Albert? She treats you like a retarded four-year-old. Stop being such a goddamned Mama's boy. Go get yourself a girlfriend. Get your own apartment. No one's going to marry you while you're living with her."

He mumbled something inaudible and slammed the door behind me. I got into the car and sat heaving for several minutes. How dared she! She had not only insulted my mother, she had manipulated me into hitting her. I couldn't believe I'd done it. I felt sick from rage and self-disgust. But the last thing I would ever do was apologize to the old witch.

On that defiant note, I put the car into gear and headed for the priory. Father Carroll was hearing confessions and would be busy for an hour. I could wait if I wanted. I declined, leaving a message that I would call later in the weekend, and headed back to the city.

I was in no mood to do anything but fight. Back at the apartment I got out my December expenses but couldn't keep my mind on them. Finally I gathered all my stale clothes and took them down to the washing machine in the basement. I changed the sheets and vacuumed and still felt terrible. At last I gave work up as a bad idea, dug my ice skates out of the closet, and drove over to the park at Montrose Harbor. They flood an outdoor rink there and I joined a crowd of children and skated with more energy than skill for over an hour. Afterward I treated myself to a late, light lunch at the Dortmunder Restaurant in the basement of the Chesterton Hotel.

It was close to three when I got home again, tired but with the anger washed out of me. The phone was ringing as I started undoing the upper of the two locks on my door. My fingers were stiff with cold; I heard the phone ring eleven times but by the time I got the bottom lock open and sprinted across the hall to the living room, the caller had hung up.

I was meeting Roger Ferrant for a movie and dinner at six. A short nap and a long bath would restore me and even leave a little time to work on my bills.

Lotty called at four, just as I had the taps running, to ask if I wanted to go with her to Uncle Stefan's tomorrow at three-thirty. We arranged for me to pick her up at three. I was lying well submerged and slightly comatose when the phone began to ring again. At first I let it go. Then, thinking it might be Ferrant calling to change plans, I leaped from the tub, trailing a cloud of Chanel bubbles behind me. But the phone had stopped again when I reached it.

Cursing the perversity of fate, I decided I had put off work long enough, got a robe and slippers, and started in earnest. By five I had my year-end statement almost complete and December's bills ready to mail to clients, and I went to change with a feeling of awesome virtue. I put on a full peasant skirt which hit me mid-calf, knee-high red cavalier boots, and a full-sleeved white blouse. Ferrant and I were meeting at the Sullivan for the six o'clock showing of *Terms of Endearment*.

He was waiting for me when I got there, a courtesy I appreciated, and kissed me enthusiastically.

I declined popcorn and Coke and we spent an agreeable two hours with half our attention on Shirley MacLaine and half on each other's bodies, making sure that various parts abandoned on Thursday morning were still where they belonged. The movie over, we agreed to complete the survey at my apartment before eating dinner.

We walked lazily up the stairs together arm in arm. I had just gotten the bottom lock unfastened when the phone started to ring again. This time I reached it by the fourth ring.

"Miss Warshawski?"

The voice was strange, a neutral voice, no accent, a hard-to-define pitch.

"Yes?"

"I'm glad to find you home at last. You're investigating the forged securities at St. Albert's, aren't you?"

"Who is this?" I demanded sharply.

"A friend, Miss Warshawski. You might almost call me an *amicus curiae*." He gave a ghostly, self-satisfied laugh. "Don't go on, Miss Warshawski. You have such beautiful gray eyes. I would hate to see them after someone poured acid on them." The line went dead.

I stood holding the phone, staring at it in disbelief. Ferrant came over to me.

"What is it, Vic?"

I put the receiver down carefully. "If you value your life, stay away from the moor at night." I tried for a light note, but my voice sounded weak even to me. Roger started to put an arm around

88

me, but I shook it off gently. "I need to think this out on my own for a minute. There's liquor and wine in the cupboard built into the dining-room wall. Why don't you fix us something?"

He went off to find drinks and I sat and looked at the phone some more. Detectives get a large volume of anonymous phone calls and letters and you'd be a quick candidate for a straitjacket if you took them very seriously. But the menace in this man's voice had been very credible. Acid in the eyes. I shivered.

I'd stirred a lot of pots and now one of them was boiling. But which one? Could poor, shriveled Aunt Rosa have gone demented and hired someone to threaten me? The idea made me laugh a little to myself and helped restore some mental balance. If not Rosa, though, it had to be the priory. And that was just as laughable. Hatfield would like to see me out of the case, but this wasn't his kind of maneuver.

Roger came in with a couple of glasses of Burgundy. "You're white, Vic. Who was that on the phone?"

I shook my head. "I wish I knew. His voice was so — so careful. Without accent. Like distilled water. Someone wants me away from the forgeries bad enough to threaten to pour acid on me."

He was shocked. "Vic! You must call the police. This is horrible." He put an arm around me. This time I didn't push him away.

"The police can't do anything, Roger. If I called and told them — do you have any idea of the number of crank calls that are made in this city in any one day?"

"But they could send someone around to keep an eye on you."

"Sure. If they didn't have eight hundred murders to investigate. And ten thousand armed robberies. And a few thousand rapes. The police can't look after me just because someone wants to make crank phone calls."

He was troubled and asked if I wanted to move in with him until things quieted down.

"Thanks, Roger. I appreciate the offer very much. But now I have someone worried enough to do something. If I stay here, I may just catch him doing it."

We'd both lost our interest in lovemaking. We finished the wine and I made us a *frittata*. Roger spent the night. I lay awake until after three, listening to his quiet, even breathing, trying to place that accentless voice, wondering who I knew who threw acid.

VIII

At the Old Forge

Sunday morning I drove the mile to Lotty's through a succession of residential one-way streets, turning often, waiting on the blind side of intersections. No one was following me. Whoever had called last night wasn't that interested. Yet.

Lotty was waiting for me in her building entryway. She looked like a little elf: five feet of compact energy wrapped in a bright green loden jacket and some kind of outlandish crimson hat. Her uncle lived in Skokie, so I went north to Irving Park Road and over to the Kennedy, the main expressway north.

As we drove past the grimy factories lining the expressway, a few snowflakes began dancing on the windshield. The cloud cover remained high, so we didn't seem to be in for a heavy storm. Turning right on the Edens fork to the northeast suburbs, I abruptly told Lotty about the phone call I'd had last night.

"It's one thing for me to risk my life just to prove a point, but it's not fair to drag you and your uncle into it as well. The odds are it was just an angry call. But if not — you need to know the risk ahead of time. And make your own decision."

91

We were approaching the Dempster interchange. Lotty told me to exit east and drive to Crawford Avenue. It wasn't until I'd followed her directions and we were moving past the imposing homes on Crawford that she answered. "I can't see that you're asking us to risk anything. You may have a problem, and it may be exacerbated by your talking to my uncle. But as long as he and I don't tell anyone you've been to see him, I don't think it'll matter. If he thinks of anything you can use — well, I would not permit you in my operating room telling me what was and what was not too great a risk. And I won't do that with you, either."

We parked in front of a quiet apartment building. Lotty's uncle met us in the doorway of his apartment. He carried his eighty-two years well, looking a bit like Laurence Olivier in *Marathon Man*. He had Lotty's bright black eyes. They twinkled as he kissed her. He half bowed, shaking hands with me.

"So. Two beautiful ladies decide to cheer up an old man's Sunday afternoon. Come in, come in." He spoke heavily accented English, unlike Lotty, who had learned it as a girl.

We followed him into a sitting room crammed with furniture and books. He ushered me ceremoniously to a stuffed chintz armchair. He and Lotty sat on a horsehair settee at a right angle to it. In front of them, on a mahogany table, was a coffee service. The silver glowed with the soft patina of age, and the coffee pot and serving pieces were decorated with fantastic creatures. I leaned forward to look at it more closely. There were griffins and centaurs, nymphs and unicorns.

Uncle Stefan beamed with pleasure at my interest. "It was made in Vienna in the early eighteenth century, when coffee was first becoming the most popular drink there." He poured cups for Lotty and me, offered me thick cream, and lifted a silver cover by its nymph-handle to reveal a plate of pastries so rich they bordered on erotic.

"Now you are not one of those ladies who eats nothing for fear of ruining her beautiful figure, are you? Good. American girls are too thin aren't they, Lottchen? You should prescribe Sacher torte for all your patients."

He continued speaking about the healthful properties of chocolate for several minutes. I drank a cup of the excellent coffee and ate a piece of hazelnut cake and wondered how to change the subject gently. However, after pouring more coffee and urging more cake on me, he abruptly took the plunge himself.

"Lotty says you wish to talk about engraving."

"Yes, sir." I told him briefly about Aunt Rosa's problems. I own a hundred shares of Acorn, a young computer company, given me in payment for an industrial espionage case I'd handled for them. I pulled the certificate out of my handbag and passed it to Uncle Stefan.

"I think most shares are printed on the same kind of paper. I'm wondering how difficult it would be to forge something like this well enough

93

to fool someone who was used to looking at them."

He took it silently and walked over to a desk that stood in front of a window. It, too, was an antique, with ornately carved legs and a green leather top. He pulled a magnifying glass from a narrow drawer in the middle, turned on a bright desk lamp, and scrutinized the certificate for more than a quarter of an hour.

"It would be difficult," he pronounced at last. "Perhaps not quite as difficult as forging paper money successfully." He beckoned me over to the desk; Lotty came, too, peering over his other shoulder. He began pointing out features of the certificate to me: The paper stock, to begin with, was a heavy-grade parchment, not easy to obtain. "And it has a characteristic weave. To fool an expert, you would need to make sure of this weave. They make the paper like this on purpose, you see, just to make the poor forger's life more difficult." He turned to grin wickedly at Lotty, who frowned in annoyance.

"Then you have the logo of the issuing company, and several signatures, each with a stamp over it. It is the stamp that is most difficult; that is almost impossible to replicate without smearing the ink of the signature. Have you seen these fake shares of your aunt's? Do you know what they did wrong?"

I shook my head. "All I know is that the serial numbers were ones that the issuing companies had never used. I don't know about these other features."

He snapped off the desk lamp and handed me back the certificate. "It's a pity you haven't seen them. Also, if you knew how the forger intended to use them, that would tell you how good, how — convincing — they had to be."

"I've thought about that. The only real use for a phony share would be as collateral. They're always examined closely by the banks at the time of sale.

"In this case, though, some real stocks were stolen. So the thief just needed to convince some priests and their auditors that they still had their assets. That way it wouldn't be like an ordinary theft where you'd know just when the stuff was taken and who had had access to it since you last saw it."

"Well, I'm sorry I can tell you nothing else, young lady. But surely you will have another piece of cake before you go."

I sat back down and took a piece of apricot-almond torte. My arteries were screaming in protest as I ate a bite. "Actually, sir, there is something else you might know. The forgeries could have been done anytime in the last ten years. But suppose, for the sake of argument, they were made relatively recently. How could I find out who did them? Assuming he — or she — worked in the Chicago area?"

He was gravely silent for a long minute. Then he spoke quietly. "Lottchen has told you about my past, how I created twenty-dollar bills. Masterpieces, really," he said with a return of his more jovial manner. "Considering I made all my own equipment.

"There are really two breeds of forger, Miss Warshawski. Independent artisans like me. And those who work for an organization. Now here you have someone who has done the work at another person's request. Unless you believe that the same person who created the new stole and disposed of the old. Really, what you want is not the — the master engraver, but his client. Am I not right?"

I nodded.

"Well, I cannot help you with finding this engraver. We independent artisans tend not to — to make public our handiwork and I am not part of a network of forgers. But perhaps I could help you find the client."

"How?" Lotty asked before I could.

"By making up such a piece and letting it be known that I have one for sale."

I thought about it. "It might work. But you'd be running a terrible risk. Even with my most persuasive intervention, it would be hard to convince the feds that your motives were pure. And remember that the people who ordered these things might be violent — I've already had a threatening phone call. If they found out you were doublecrossing them, their justice would be even harder to take than a stint at Fort Leavenworth."

Uncle Stefan leaned over and clasped one of my hands. "Young lady, I am an old man. Although I enjoy life, my fear of death has passed. And such an occupation would be rejuvenating for me."

Lotty interrupted with some vigorous arguments of her own. Their discussion got quite heated and moved into German, until Lotty said disgustedly in English, "On your grave we will put a marker reading 'He died stubborn.'"

After that, Uncle Stefan and I discussed practical details. He would need to keep my Acorn certificate and get some others. He would find any supplies he needed and send me the bills. To be on the safe side, in case my anonymous caller really meant business, he wouldn't phone me. If he needed to talk to me, he'd run an ad in the *Herald-Star*. Unfortunately, he couldn't promise very speedy results.

"You must resign yourself to weeks, perhaps many weeks, not days, my dear Miss Warshawski."

Lotty and I left amid mutual protestations of goodwill — at least between Uncle Stefan and me. Lotty was a little frosty. As we got into the car she said, "I suppose I could call you in to consult on geriatric cases. You could think of criminal enterprises that would bring adventure and the flush of youth back to people worried about making ends meet on Social Security."

I drove over to Route 41, the old highway connecting Chicago and the North Shore. Nowadays it offered a quiet, pretty drive past stately homes and the lake. "I'm sorry, Lotty. I didn't go there with anything more than the hope that your uncle might know who's who in Chicago forging. Personally, I think his idea is a long shot. If he can do the job and make some contacts, how likely is it he'll come up with the right people? But it's a clever idea, and better than anything I can think of. Anyway, I'd certainly rather have a charming criminal as my only Chicago relative than an honest bitch; if you're too upset, I'll trade you Rosa for Stefan."

Lotty laughed at that and we made the drive back to Chicago peaceably, stopping on the far North Side for a Thai dinner. I dropped Lotty at her apartment and went on home to call my answering service. A Father Carroll had phoned, and so, too, had Murray Ryerson from the *Star*.

I tried the priory first. "They told me you were by here yesterday, Miss Warshawski. I'm sorry I couldn't see you then. I don't know if you've heard, but we had some rather extraordinary news this morning: We found the original certificates."

I stood momentarily stunned. "That *is* extraordinary," I finally said. "Where did they turn up?"

"They were on the altar this morning when we began celebrating mass." Since well over a hundred people had legitimate business in the priory chapel on Sunday mornings, no one could possibly say who might or might not have gone there early and returned the stolen goods. Yes, the FBI had sent someone out to take possession, but Hatfield had called at three to say that these shares were genuine. The FBI was keeping them awhile to run lab tests on them. And Carroll didn't know now if they'd ever get them back.

Out of curiosity I asked if Rosa had been to mass that morning. Yes, and looking grimly at anyone who tried to talk to her, Carroll assured me. Her son stayed away, but he usually did. As we started to hang up, he remembered my question about whether anyone at the priory had talked to Rosa about pulling out of the investigation. He had asked the fathers whom Rosa would most likely listen to and none of them had talked to her.

I called Murray next. He wasn't as full of the returned certificates as I expected. More recent news occupied his attention.

"I talked to Hatfield twenty minutes ago. You know what an arrogant, uncommunicative bastard he is. Well, I couldn't get shit out of him about the returned stocks and I asked every question in my arsenal and more besides. I got him in a corner finally and he as good as admitted the FBI is dropping the investigation. Putting it on the back burner, he said, cliché hack that he is. But that means dropping it."

"Well, if the real things have turned up, they don't need to worry so much."

"Yeah, and I believe in the Easter bunny. Come on, Vic!"

"Okay, wordly-wise newspaperman. Who's applying the screws? The FBI isn't scared of anyone except maybe J. Edgar's ghost. If you think someone's backing them off, who is it?"

"Vic, you don't believe that any more than I do. No organization is exempt from pressure if you know where the right nerves are. If you know something you're not telling I'll — I'll — " he broke off, unable to think of an effective threat. "And another thing. What was that crap you gave me about your poor frail old aunt? I sent one of my babies out to talk to her yesterday afternoon and some fat goon who claimed he was the son practically broke my gal's foot in the door. Then the Vignelli woman joined him in the hall and treated her to some high-level swearing on newspapers in general and the *Star* in particular."

I laughed softly. "Okay, Rosa! Two points for our side."

"Goddamn it, Vic, why'd you sic me onto her?"

"I don't know," I said irritably. "To see if she'd be as nasty to anyone else as she is to me? To see if you could learn something she wouldn't tell me? I don't know. I'm sorry your poor little protégée had her feelings hurt, but she's going to have to learn to take it if she plans to survive in your game." I started to tell Murray that I, too, had been warned off the investigation, then held back. Maybe someone had brushed back the FBI. And maybe that someone had called me as well. If the FBI respected them, so should I. I bade Murray an absentminded good-night and hung up.

IX

Final Trade

The snow held off overnight. I got up late to do my virtuous five miles, running north and west through the neighborhood. I didn't think anyone was watching me, but if they were, it was sensible to vary my route.

A little later I followed the same procedure in my car, looping the Omega north and west through the side streets, then hitting the Kennedy from the west at Lawrence. I seemed to be clean. Thirty miles south on the expressway, past the city limits, is the town of Hazel Crest. You cannot buy handguns in Chicago, but a number of suburbs do a flourishing legal business in them. At Riley's, on 161st Street, I showed them my private investigator's license and my certificate that proved I'd passed the state's exam for private security officers. These enabled me to waive the three-day waiting period and also to register the gun in Chicago; private citizens can't register handguns here unless they bought them before 1979.

I spent the rest of the day finishing up a few outstanding problems — serving a subpoena to a bank vice-president hiding unconvincingly in Rosemont, and showing a small jewelry store how to install a security system.

And I kept wondering who was backing off first Rosa and then the FBI. It wouldn't help to park in front of Rosa's and watch her. What I really needed was a tap on her phone. And that was beyond my resources.

I tried thinking about it from the other end. Who had I talked to? That was easy: the prior, the procurator, and the student master. I'd also told Ferrant and Agnes what I was doing. None of these five seemed a likely candidate for threatening either me or the FBI.

Of course, Jablonski could be that type of anti-abortion fanatic who thinks it's a worse sin to have an abortion than to kill someone who promotes freedom of choice, but he hadn't struck me as particularly crazy. Despite Pelly's protests, the Catholic Church does carry a lot of clout in Chicago. But even if it could pressure the FBI out of the investigation, why would it want to? Anyway, a priory in Melrose Park was on the fringes of the Church power structure. And why would they steal their own stock certificates? Even assuming they were in touch with forgers the whole idea was too far out. I went back to my original theory — my phone call had come from a crank, and the FBI was backing out because it was understaffed and overworked.

Nothing happened to make me change my mind during the next several days. I wondered vaguely how Uncle Stefan was doing. If it weren't for the fact that there really had been a forgery, I would have put the whole thing out of my mind.

102

On Wednesday I had to go to Elgin to testify in a case being tried in the state appeals court there. I stopped in Melrose Park on my way back to town, partly to see Carroll, partly to see if a visit to the priory might tickle my threatening caller back to life. If it didn't, it would prove nothing. But if I heard from him again, it might show he was watching the priory.

It was four-thirty when I reached St. Albert's, and the friars were filing into the chapel for vespers and evening mass. Father Carroll came out of his office as I stood hesitating and gave me a welcoming smile, inviting me to join them for evening prayer.

I followed him into the chapel. Two rows of raised stalls faced each other in the middle of the room. I went with him to the back row on the left side. The seats were divided by arms raised between them. I sat down and slid back in the seat. Father Carroll gave me a service book and quietly pointed out the lessons and prayers they would be using, then knelt to pray.

In the winter twilight, I felt as though I had slipped back five or six centuries in time. The brothers in their white robes, the candlelight flickering on the simple wooden altar to my left, the few people coming in from the outside to worship in the public space divided from the main chapel by a carved wooden screen — all evoked the medieval Church. I was the discordant note in my black wool suit, my high heels, my makeup.

Father Carroll led the service, singing in a clear,

103

well-trained voice. The whole service was sung antiphonally between the two banks of stalls. It's true, as Rosa said, that I'm no Christian, but I found the service satisfying.

Afterward, Carroll invited me back to his office for tea. Almost all tea tastes like stewed alfalfa to me, but I politely drank a cup of the pale green brew and asked him if he'd heard anything more from the FBI.

"They tested the shares for fingerprints and a lot of other things — I don't know what. They thought there might be dust or something on them that would show where the things had been stored. I guess they didn't find anything, so they're going to bring them back tomorrow." He grinned mischievously. "I'm making them give me an armed escort over to the Bank of Melrose Park. We're getting those things into a bank vault."

He asked me to stay for dinner, which was being served in five minutes. Memories of Kraft American cheese restrained me. On an impulse I invited him to eat with me in Melrose Park. The town has a couple of excellent Italian restaurants. Somewhat surprised, he accepted.

"I'll just change out of my robe." He smiled again. "The young brothers like to go out in them in public — they like people to look at them and know they're seeing a foreign breed. But we older men lose our taste for showing off."

He returned in ten minutes in a plaid sport shirt, black slacks, and a black jacket. We had a pleasant meal at one of the little restaurants on North Avenue. We talked about singing; I complimented him on his voice and learned he'd been a student at the American Conservatory before entering the priesthood. He asked me about my work and I tried to think of some interesting cases.

"I guess the payoff is you get to be your own boss. And you have the satisfaction of solving problems, even if they're only little problems most of the time. I was just out in Elgin today, testifying at the state court there. It brought back my early days with the Chicago public defender's office. Either we had to defend maniacs who ought to have been behind bars for the good of the world at large, or we had poor chumps who were caught in the system and couldn't buy their way out. You'd leave court every day feeling as though you'd just helped worsen the situation. As a detective, if I can get at the truth of a problem, I feel as though I've made some contribution."

"I see. Not a glamorous occupation, but it sounds very worthwhile. . . . I'd never heard Mrs. Vignelli mention you. Until she called last week, I didn't know she had any family besides her son. Are there other relatives?"

I shook my head. "My mother was her only Chicago relative — my grandfather and she were brother and sister. There may be some family on my Uncle Carl's side. He died years before I was born. Shot himself, actually — very sad for Rosa." I fiddled with the stem on my wineglass, tempted to ask him if he knew what lay behind Rosa's dark insinuations about Gabriella. But even if he knew, he probably wouldn't tell me. And it seemed vulgar to bring up the family enmity in public.

After I took him back to the priory I swung onto the Eisenhower back to Chicago. A little light snow had begun falling. It was a few minutes before ten; I turned on WBBM, Chicago's news station, to catch news and a weather forecast.

I listened vaguely to reports of failed peace initiatives in Lebanon, continued high unemployment, poor retail sales in December despite Christmas shopping. Then Alan Swanson's crisp voice continued:

> Tonight's top local story is the violent death of a Chicago stockbroker. Cleaning woman Martha Gonzales found the body of broker Agnes Paciorek in one of the conference rooms in the offices of Feldstein, Holtz and Woods, where Miss Paciorek worked. She had been shot twice in the head. Police have not ruled out suicide as a cause of death. CBS news correspondent Mark Weintraub is with Sergeant McGonnigal at the Fort Dearborn Tower offices of Feldstein, Holtz and Woods.

Swanson switched over to Weintraub. I almost swerved into a ditch at Cicero Avenue. My hands were shaking and I pulled the car over to the side. I turned off the engine. Semis roared past, rattling the little Omega. The car cooled, and my feet began growing numb inside their pumps. "Two

106

shots in the head and the police still haven't ruled out suicide," I muttered. My voice jarred me back to myself; I turned the motor on and headed back into the city at a sober pace.

WBBM played the story at ten-minute intervals, with few new details. The bullets were from a twenty-two-caliber pistol. The police finally decided to eliminate suicide since no gun was found by the body. Miss Paciorek's purse had been recovered from a locked drawer in her desk. I heard Sergeant McGonnigal saying in a voice made scratchy by static that someone must have intended to rob her, then killed her in a rage because she didn't have a purse.

On impulse I drove north to Addison and stopped in front of Lotty's apartment. It was almost eleven: no lights showed. Lotty gets her sleep when she can — her practice involves a lot of night emergencies. My trouble would keep.

Back at my own apartment, I changed from my suit into a quilted robe and sat down in the living room with a glass of Black Label whiskey. Agnes and I went back a long way together, back to the Golden Age of the sixties, when we thought love and energy would end racism and sexism. She'd come from a wealthy family, her father a heart surgeon at one of the big suburban hospitals. They'd fought her about her friends, her life-style, her ambitions, and she'd won every battle. Relations with her mother became more and more strained. I would have to call Mrs. Paciorek, who disliked me since I represented everything she didn't want Agnes to be. I'd have to hear how they always knew this would happen, working downtown where the niggers are. I drank another glass of whiskey.

I'd forgotten all about laying some bait for my anonymous phone caller until the telephone interrupted my maudlin mood. I jumped slightly and looked at my watch: eleven-thirty. I picked up a Dictaphone from my desk and turned it to "Record" before picking up the receiver.

It was Roger Ferrant, feeling troubled about Agnes's death. He'd seen it on the ten o'clock news and tried calling me then. We commiserated a bit; then he said hesitantly, "I feel responsible for her death."

The whiskey was fogging my brain slightly. "What'd you do — send a punk up to the sixtieth floor of the Fort Dearborn Tower?" I switched off the Dictaphone and sat down.

"Vic, I don't need your tough-girl act. I feel responsible because she was staying late working on this possible Ajax takeover. It wasn't something she had time for during the day. If I hadn't called her — "

"If you hadn't called her, she would have been there late working on another project," I interrupted him coldly. "Agnes often finished her day late — the lady worked hard. And if it comes to that, you wouldn't have called her if I hadn't given you her number, so if anyone's responsible, it's me." I took another swallow of whiskey. "And I won't believe that."

We hung up. I finished my third glass of scotch and put the bottle away in the built-in cupboard in the dining room, draped my robe over a chair back, and climbed naked into bed. Just as I turned out the bedside light, something Ferrant had said rang a bell with me. I called him back on the bedside phone.

"It's me, Vic. How did you know Agnes was working late on your project tonight?"

"I talked to her this afternoon. She said she was going to stay late and talk to some of her broker pals; she didn't have time to get to it during the day."

"In person or on the phone?"

"Huh? Oh, I don't know." He thought about it. "I can't remember exactly what she said. But it left me with the impression that she was planning to see someone in person."

"You should talk to the police, Roger." I hung up and fell asleep almost immediately.

X

Mixed Grill

No matter how often I wake up with a headache, I never remember it the next time I'm putting away five or six ounces of whiskey. Thursday morning a dry mouth and pounding head and heart woke me at five-thirty. I looked disgustedly at myself in the bathroom mirror. "You're getting old, V.I., and unattractive. When your face has cracks in it the morning after five ounces of scotch, it's time to stop drinking."

I squeezed some fresh orange juice and drank it in one long swallow, took four aspirins, and went back to bed. The ringing phone woke me again at eight-thirty. A neutral young male voice said he was connected with Lieutenant Robert Mallory of the Chicago police department and would I be able to come downtown that morning and talk to the lieutenant.

"It's always a pleasure for me to talk to Lieutenant Mallory," I replied formally, if somewhat thickly, through the miasma of sleep. "Perhaps you could tell me what this is about."

The neutral young man didn't know, but if I was free at nine-thirty, the lieutenant would see me then.

My next call was to the *Herald-Star*. Murray

Ryerson hadn't yet come in for the day. I called his apartment, and felt vindictive pleasure at getting him out of bed. "Murray, what do you know about Agnes Paciorek?"

He was furious. "I can't believe you got me out of bed to ask me that. Go buy the fucking morning edition." He slammed the phone down.

Angry myself, I dialed again. "Listen, Ryerson. Agnes Paciorek was one of my oldest friends. She got shot last night. Now Bobby Mallory wants to talk to me. I'm sure he's not calling for deep background on University Women United, or Clergy and Laity Concerned About Vietnam. What was in her office that makes him want to see me?"

"Hang on a second." He put the receiver down; I could hear his feet padding away down the hall, then water running and a woman's voice saying something indistinguishable. I ran into the kitchen and put a small pot of water on the stove, ground beans for one cup of coffee, and brought cup, water, and filter back to my bedside phone — all before Murray returned.

"I hope you can hold off Jessica or whatever her name is for a few seconds."

"Don't be catty, Vic. It isn't attractive." I heard springs creaking, then a muffled "ouch" from Murray.

"Right," I said dryly. "Now tell me about Agnes."

Paper rustled, springs creaked again, and Murray's smothered voice whispered, "Knock it off, Alice." Then he put the mouthpiece in front of his lips again and began reading from his notes.

"Agnes Paciorek was shot at about eight last night. Two twenty-two bullets in the brain. Office doors not locked — cleaning women lock behind when they finish sixtieth floor, usually at eleven o'clock. Martha Gonzales cleans floors fifty-seven through sixty, got to floor at her usual time, nine-fifteen, saw nothing unusual on premises, got to conference room at nine-thirty, saw body, called police. No personal attack — no signs of rape or struggle. Police presume attacker took her completely by surprise or possibly someone she knew. . . . That's the lot. You're someone she knew. They probably just want to know where you were at eight last night. By the way, since you're on the phone, where were you?"

"In a bar, waiting for a report from my hired gun." I hung up and looked sourly around the room. The orange juice and aspirin had dissipated the headache, but I felt rotten. I wasn't going to have time for running if I had to be in Mallory's office by nine-thirty, and a long, slow run was what I needed to get the poisons out of my system. I didn't even have time for a long bath, so I steamed myself under the shower for ten minutes, put on the crepe de chine pantsuit, this time with a man-tailored shirt of pale lemon, and ran down the stairs two at a time to my car.

If the Warshawski family has a motto, which I doubt, it's "Never skip a meal," perhaps in Old Church Slavonic, wreathed around a dinner plate with knife and fork rampant. At any rate, I stopped at a bakery on Halsted for coffee and a ham croissant and headed for Lake Shore Drive and the Loop. The croissant was stale, and the ham might have been rancid, but I plowed into it bravely. Bobby's little chats can go on for hours. I wanted to fortify myself.

Lieutenant Mallory had joined the police the same year as my dad. But my father, his better in brains, never had a lot of ambition, certainly not enough to buck the prejudice against Polish cops in an all-Irish world. So Mallory had risen and Tony had stayed on the beat, but the two remained good friends. That's why Mallory hates talking to me about crime. He thinks Tony Warshawski's daughter should be making a better world by producing happy healthy babies, not by catching desperadoes.

I pulled into the visitors' parking lot at the Eleventh Street station at nine-twenty-three. I sat in the car to relax for a few minutes, finish my coffee, clear my mind of all thoughts. For once, I had no guilty secrets. It should be a straightforward conversation.

At nine-thirty I made my way past the high wooden admissions desk where pimps were lining up to redeem last night's haul of hookers, and went down the hallway to Mallory's office. The place smelled a lot like St. Albert's priory. Must be the linoleum floors. Or maybe all the people in uniform.

Mallory was on the phone when I got to the cubicle he calls an office. His shirt sleeves were

113

rolled up and the muscular arm that waved me in strained the white fabric. Before entering, I helped myself to coffee from a pot in the corner of the hall, then sat in an uncomfortable folding chair across the desk while he finished his call. Mallory's face betrays his moods. He turns red and blustery on days when I'm on the periphery of some crime; relaxed and genial means he's thinking of me as his old buddy Tony's daughter. Today he looked at me gravely as he hung up the phone. Trouble. I took a swallow of coffee and waited.

He flicked a switch on the intercom on his desk and waited silently while someone answered his summons. A young black officer, resembling Neil Washington from *Hill Street Blues*, came in shortly with a steno pad in one hand and a cup of coffee for Mallory in the other. Mallory introduced him as Officer Tarkinton.

"Miss Warshawski is a private investigator," Mallory informed Tarkinton, spelling the name for him. "Officer Tarkinton is going to keep a record of our conversation."

The formality and the display of officialdom were supposed to intimidate. I drank some more coffee, puzzled.

"Were you a friend of Agnes Marie Paciorek?"

"Bobby, you're making me feel like I ought to have my attorney here. What's going on?"

"Just answer the questions. We'll get to the reasons quickly enough."

"My relations with Agnes aren't a secret. You

can get the details from anyone who knows both of us. Unless you tell me what's behind this, I'm not answering any questions."

"When did you first meet Agnes Paciorek?"

I drank some more coffee and said nothing.

"You and Paciorek are described as sharing an alternate life-style. This same witness says you are responsible for introducing the dead woman to unconventional behavior. Do you want to comment on that?"

I felt my temper rising and controlled it with an effort. It's a typical police tactic in this type of interrogation — get the witness mad enough to start mouthing off. And who knows what self-constructed pitfalls you'll wander into? I used to see it all the time in the public defender's office. I counted to ten in Italian and waited.

Mallory clenched his fist tightly around the edge of his metal desk. "You and Paciorek were lesbians, weren't you?" Suddenly his control broke and he smashed his fist on the desk top. "When Tony was dying you were up at the University of Chicago screwing around like a pervert, weren't you? It wasn't enough that you demonstrated against the war and got involved with that filthy abortion underground. Don't think we couldn't have pulled you in on that. We could have, a hundred times over. But everyone wanted to protect Tony. You were the most important thing in the world to him, and all the time — Jesus Christ, Victoria. When I talked to Mrs. Paciorek this morning, I wanted to puke."

115

"Are you charging me with something, Bobby?" He sat smoldering.

"Because if you're not, I'm leaving." I got up, putting an empty Styrofoam cup on the corner of the desk, and started out the door.

"No you don't, young lady. Not until we get this straightened out."

"There's nothing to straighten out," I said coldly. "First of all, under the Illinois criminal code, lesbianism between consenting adults is not an indictable offense. Therefore it is none of your goddamned business whether or not Ms. Paciorek and I were lovers. Second, my relations with her are totally unconnected with your murder investigation. Unless you can demonstrate some kind of connection, I have absolutely nothing to say to you."

We locked gazes for an angry minute. Then Bobby, his face still set in hurt hard lines, asked Officer Tarkinton to leave. When we were alone he said in a tight voice, "I should have gotten someone else to handle the interrogation. But goddamn it, Vicki . . ."

His voice trailed off. I was still angry, but I felt a little grudging sympathy for him. "You know, Bobby, what hurts me is that you talk to Mrs. Paciorek, whom you never met before in your life, and believe a shopping list of calumny from her without even asking me, and you've known me since I was born."

"Okay, talk. I'm asking. Talk to me about the Paciorek girl."

I picked up the Styrofoam cup and looked inside. It was still empty. "Agnes and I met when we were both students in the college. I was prelaw and she was a math major who ultimately decided to get an MBA. I'm not going to try to describe to you what it felt like in those days — you don't have much sympathy for the causes that consumed us. I think sometimes that I'll never feel so — so alive again."

A wave of bittersweet memory swept over me and I closed my eyes tightly to keep tears at bay. "Then the dream started falling apart. We had Watergate and drugs and the deteriorating economy, and racism and sexual discrimination continued despite our enthusiasm. So we all settled down to deal with reality and earn a living. You know my story. I guess my ideals died the hardest. It's often that way with the children of immigrants. We need to buy the dream so bad we sometimes can't wake up.

"Well, Agnes's story was a little different. You met the parents. First of all, her father is a successful cardiac surgeon, pulls in a good half million a year at a conservative guess. But more important, her mother is one of the Savages. You know, old Catholic money. Convent of the Sacred Heart for prep school, then the deb balls and all the other stuff. I don't know exactly how the very rich live, just differently from you and me.

"Anyway, Agnes was born fighting it. She fought it through twelve years at Sacred Heart, and came to the U of C against their harshest opposition.

She borrowed the money because they wouldn't pay to send her to a Jewish commie school. So it wasn't too surprising that she got swept up in all the causes of the sixties. And for both of us, feminism was the most important, because it was central to us."

I was talking more to myself than to Bobby; I wasn't sure how much he could really hear of what I was saying.

"Well, after Tony died, Agnes used to invite me up to Lake Forest for Christmas and I got to know the Pacioreks. And Mrs. Paciorek decided to hang all Agnes's weird behavior on me. It took her off the hook, you see — she wasn't a failure as a parent. Agnes, who figured as sweet and impressionable in this scenario, had fallen under my evil influence.

"Well, buy that or not as you choose, but keep in mind that sweet impressionable people don't build up the kind of brokerage business Agnes did.

"Anyway, Agnes and I were good friends at the University. And we stayed good friends. And in its way that was a small miracle. When our rap group followed the national trend and split between radical lesbians and, well, straights, she became a lesbian and I didn't. But we remained very good friends — an achievement for that era, when politics divided marriages and friends alike. It seems pointless now, but it was very real then."

Like a lot of my friends, I'd resented suddenly being labeled straight because of my sexual preferences. After all, we'd been fighting the straights

— the prowar, antiabortion, racist world. Now overnight we were straights, too? It all seems senseless now. The older I get, the less politics means to me. The only thing that seems to matter is friendship. And Agnes and I had been good friends for a long time. I could feel tears behind my eyes and squeezed them tightly again. When I looked up at Bobby he was frowning at the desk top, drawing circles on it with the back of a ball-point pen.

"Well, I've told you my story, Bobby. Now explain why you needed to hear it."

He continued to stare at the desk. "Where were you last night?"

My temper began rising again. "Goddamn it, if you want to charge me with murder, come out and do it. I'm not accounting for my movements otherwise."

"From the way the body looked, we believe she was seeing someone she expected, not a chance intruder." He pulled a leather-covered date book from the middle desk drawer. He flipped it open and tossed it to me. For Wednesday, January 18, Agnes had written; "V.I.W.," heavily underscored, followed by several exclamation points.

"Looks like a date, doesn't it." I tossed the book back to him. "Have you established that I'm her only acquaintance with those initials?"

"There aren't too many people in the metropolitan area with those initials."

"So the current theory reads that she and I were lovers and we had a falling-out? Now she's been living with Phyllis Lording for three years and I've been involved with God-knows-who-all since we left school, besides being married once — oh, yeah, I guess the theory would say I divorced Dick to keep Agnes happy. But despite all that, suddenly we decided to have a grand lovers' quarrel and because I'm trained in self-defense and carry a gun at times, I won by putting a couple of bullets through her head. You said hearing about me from Mrs. Paciorek made you want to puke; frankly, Bobby, listening to what goes on in the alleged minds of the police makes me feel like I've wandered into a really low-grade porn shop. Talk about puking . . . Anything else you want to know?" I stood up again.

"Well, you tell me why she wanted to see you. And were you there last night?"

I stayed on my feet. "You should have started with your last question. I was in Melrose Park last night with the Reverend Boniface Carroll, O.P., Prior of St. Albert's Dominican Priory, from about four-thirty to about ten. And I don't know why Agnes wanted to talk to me — assuming I'm the one she wanted to talk to. Try Vincent Ignatius Williams."

"Who's he?" Bobby demanded, startled.

"I don't know. But his initials are V.I.W." I turned and left, ignoring Bobby's voice as it came bellowing down the corridor after me. I was furious; my hands were shaking with rage. I stood by the door of the Omega taking in deep gulps of icy air, slowly expelling it, trying to calm myself.

Finally I climbed into the car. The dashboard clock read eleven. I headed the Omega north into the Loop, parking at a public lot not too far from the Pulteney. From there I walked three blocks to Ajax's headquarters.

Their glass-and-steel skyscraper occupies sixty of the ugliest stories in Chicago. Located at the northwestern corner of Michigan and Adams, it overwhelms the Art Institute opposite. I've often wondered why the Blairs and the McCormicks allowed a monster like Ajax so near their favorite charity.

Uniformed security guards patrol Ajax's gray lobby. Their job is to keep miscreants like me from attacking officers like Roger Ferrant. Even after they'd checked with him and found he was willing to see me, they made me fill out a form for a visitor's pass. By that time my temper was so brittle that I scribbled a note under my signature promising not to mug any of their executives in the hallway.

Ferrant's office lay on the lake side of the fifty-eighth floor, which proved the importance of his temporary position.

An angular secretary in a large antechamber informed me that Mr. Ferrant was engaged and would see me shortly. Her desk, facing the open door, kept her from seeing Lake Michigan. I wondered if that was her own idea, or if Ajax management didn't think secretaries could be trusted to work if they saw the outside world.

I sat in a large, green-covered plush armchair

and flicked through the morning's *Wall Street Journal* while I waited. The headline in "Heard on the Street" caught my eye. The *Journal* had picked up the rumor of a potential takeover for Ajax. The Tisch brothers and other likely insurance-company owners had been interviewed, but all of them professed total ignorance. Ajax chairman Gordon Firth was quoted as saying:

> Naturally we're watching the share price with interest, but no one has approached our shareholders with a friendly offer.

And that seemed to be all they knew in New York.

At a quarter of twelve the door to the inner office opened. A group of middle-aged men, mostly overweight, came out talking in a subdued hubbub. Ferrant followed, straightening his tie with one hand and pushing his hair out of his eyes with the other. He smiled, but his thin face was troubled.

"Have you eaten? Good. We'll go to the executive dining room on sixty."

I told him that was fine and waited while he put on his suit jacket. We rode in silence to the top of the building.

In the executive dining and meeting rooms, Ajax compensated for the stark unfriendliness of the lobby. Brocade drapes were looped back over gauze hangings at the windows. Walls were paneled in dark wood, possibly mahogany, and the recessed lighting picked up strategically placed bits of modern sculpture and painting.

Ferrant had his own table near a window, with plenty of space between him and any eavesdropping neighbors. As soon as we were seated, a black-uniformed waiter popped out of the ground to waft luncheon menus in front of us and ask for our drink orders. Last night's scotch was adding to the discomfort of my morning with Mallory. I ordered orange juice. I flipped indifferently through the menu. When the waiter came back with our drinks, I found I didn't have any appetite.

"Nothing for me now."

Ferrant looked at his watch and said apologetically that he was on a short timetable and would have to eat.

Once the waiter was gone, I said abruptly, "I spent the morning with the police. They think Agnes was expecting someone last night. You said the same thing. Did she tell you anything — anything at all that would help identify the one she was waiting for?"

"Barrett sent me the names of brokers here in Chicago who've been trading in Ajax. It came in Monday's mail and I met Agnes for lunch on Tuesday and gave it to her then, along with the list of those the shares had been registered to. She said she knew a partner in one of the firms pretty well and would call him. But she didn't tell me who."

"Did you keep a copy of the names?"

He shook his head. "I've kicked myself a hundred times over for that. But I don't have the

American photocopy habit. I always thought it was stupid, generated mounds of useless paper. Now I'm changing my mind. I can get Barrett to send me another copy, but I won't get it today."

I drummed my fingers on the table. Useless to be irritated about that. "Maybe her secretary can dig it up for me. When she talked to you yesterday, did she mention my name at all?"

He shook his head. "Should she have?"

"She had my initials in her date book. With Agnes, that means — meant — a reminder to herself. She didn't write down her appointments; she relied on her secretary to keep track of them. So my initials meant she wanted to talk to me." I'd been too angry with Mallory to explain that to him, too angry, as well, to tell him about Ferrant and Ajax.

"The police came up with an extraterrestrial theory about Agnes and me being lovers and my shooting her out of spite or revenge or something. It didn't make me too confiding. But I can't help wondering. . . . You saw the story in this morning's *Journal*?"

He nodded.

"Well, here you've got a possible takeover bid. None of the principals — if there are any — step into the open. Agnes starts prying. She wants to talk to me, but before she does that she ends up dead."

He looked startled. "You don't really think her death has anything to do with Ajax, do you?"

The waiter brought him a club sandwich and

he began eating automatically. "It really troubles me to think my questions might have sent that poor girl to her death. You pooh-poohed me last night for feeling responsible. Christ! I feel ten times as responsible now." He put his sandwich down and leaned across the table. "Vic, no company takeover is more valuable than a person's life. Leave it be. If there is a connection — if you stir up the same people — I just couldn't bear it. It's bad enough to feel responsible for Agnes. I scarcely knew her. But I just don't want to worry about that with you, too."

You can't touch someone in the executive dining room; every corporate officer I ever met was a born-again gossip. Word would spread through all sixty floors by nightfall that Roger Ferrant had brought his girlfriend to lunch and held hands with her.

"Thanks, Roger. Agnes and I — we're grown women. We make our own mistakes. No one else has to take responsibility for them. I'm always careful. I think you owe taking care of yourself to the friends who love you, and I don't want to cause my friends any grief. . . . I'm not sure I believe in immortality or heaven or any of those things. But I do believe, with Roger Fox, that we all have to listen to the voice within us, and how easily you can look at yourself in the mirror depends on whether you obey that voice or not. Everyone's voice gives different counsel, but you can only interpret the one you hear."

He finished his drink before answering. "Well,

Vic, add me to the list of friends who don't want to grieve over you." He got up abruptly and headed for the exit, leaving his sandwich half eaten on the table.

XI

Acid Test

The Fort Dearborn Trust, Chicago's largest bank, has buildings on each of the four corners of Monroe and LaSalle. The Tower, their most recent construction, is a seventy-five-story building on the southwest side of the intersection. Its curved, aqua-tinted glass sides represent the newest trend in Chicago architecture. The elevator banks are built around a small jungle. I skirted trees and creeping vines until I found the elevators to the sixtieth floor, where Feldstein, Holtz and Woods, the firm in which Agnes had been a partner, occupied the north half. I'd first been there when the firm moved in three years ago. Agnes had just been made a partner and Phyllis Lording and I were helping her hang pictures in her enormous new office.

Phyllis taught English at the University of Illinois — Chicago Circle. I'd called her from the Ajax dining room before coming over to the Fort Dearborn Tower. It was a painful conversation, Phyllis trying unsuccessfully not to cry. Mrs. Paciorek was refusing to tell her anything about the funeral arrangements.

"If you're not married, you don't have any rights when your lover dies," she said bitterly.

I promised to come see her that evening and asked if Agnes had said anything, either about Ajax or why she wanted to see me.

"She told me she'd had lunch with you last Friday, you and some Englishman. . . . I know she said he'd brought up an interesting problem. . . . I just can't remember anything else now."

If Phyllis didn't know, Agnes's secretary might. I hadn't bothered phoning ahead to Feldstein, Holtz and Woods, and I arrived on a scene of extraordinary chaos. The inside of a brokerage firm always looks like a hurricane's just been through; brokers carve perilous perches for themselves inside mountains of documents — prospectuses, research reports, annual reports. The wonder is that they ever work through enough paper to know anything about the companies they trade in.

A murder investigation superimposed on this fire hazard was unbearable, even for someone with my housekeeping standards. Gray dusting powder covered the few surfaces not crowded with paper. Desks and terminals were jammed into the already overflowing space so work could go on while police cordoned off parts of the floor they thought might yield clues.

As I walked through the open area toward Agnes's office, a young patrolman stopped me, demanding my business. "I have an account here. I'm going to see my broker." He tried to stop me with further questions, but someone barked an order at him from the other side of the room